BRAMDEN HOUSE

ECHOES

DARCIE MCGRATH

ECHOES

DARCIE MCGRATH

ISBN: 979-8-9892451-3-0

Although some of the events in this book are inspired by true events, and contain certain places and events within historical narrative, the book is a work of fiction, and the places and characters within are of the writer's imagination only, and are not based on any individuals, living or dead.

To my teachers, mentors, and friends that have taught me so

much......and to "Harold" who taught me more

Prologue

Bentonsport, Iowa, USA

A lone shriek split the silence of the moonless night, as the chalk-white doors of the three-story Federalist-style house ejected the house's occupant onto the pavement below the entryway steps. The lanky, curly-haired man landed, unceremoniously, on the rough-hewn cement. His nose was scant inches from a serious impact with the ground. Luckily for him, he chose his cartoon ghost long-sleeve pajamas to wear that night; albeit a bit juvenile, it kept him warm as he lay on the cold cement and protected his body from any serious scrapes. He supposed he should feel doubly-grateful the streets of the small rural town tended to roll up early on a week night, but it was still humiliating that the house would do this to him, again, for the third time this week.

Breathe, breathe, breathe! Peter Elgin thought, grounding his bodily energy into the cool concrete beneath his palms.

This was enough. This was more than *enough*.

The house made it clear that it did not like him, and was, for certain, *not* living up to expectations. Over the last several months, the paranormal researcher had to deal with the harshness of the Midwest polar vortexes with less than adequate modern insulation. Even though many of the floors were equipped with fireplaces, it did next to nothing to correct the temperature within the domicile.

Because of its isolated location, it made the house, very much, a destination location. The unincorporated township status made regular snow removal from the rustic streets an unreliable event. He could only add those things to the list of unattractive features for his paranormal investigator audience.

And then, there was the presence of the paranormal activity itself. Since his acquisition of the property, the activity in the house seemed almost to *ghost* him. His soft-launch of promoting the business as a ghost-hunting mecca fell flat with many of his high-profile clients leaving frustrated when the entities of the house failed to…well…*perform* as expected. Even though the house seemed more than active during his expedition last Fall, the house had fallen, eerily, silent when other investigators would arrive. Considering that his mortgage was dependent on the property becoming a paranormal attraction, he found himself begging and cajoling the entities to come out and play. When that produced less-than-desired activity, he began to provoke with haughty language and threats.

As he considered his prone position on the pavement in front of the house, he was ready to entertain the idea that he might have made a mistake with that approach. The swearing and the taunting method that had so colored his career seemed to only produce effect when he was in the house. Alone. At night. And not pleasantly.

Since he was the only one experiencing it, it gave spread to gossip among his investigator customers that he might have been greatly exaggerating the house's activity. Adding that to the list of other issues, he was hemorrhaging money, quickly. He was running out of options.

He felt the firm lump under his body and realized, to his relief and consternation that he had bolted out of the house with his cell phone in hand. Well, at least it was functional and, in his hand, until he landed on it.

Hitting the power button to illuminate the screen, he managed to activate the contacts list and thumb-scroll, single-handedly until he found the one number he was looking for. Awkwardly pressing the device against his ear, the line rang its usual electronic tattoo. He appeared to have an ounce of luck left in that they appeared to have a night-time answering service. Doing his best to make his restricted breathing sound normal, he muttered in to the device.

"Andrew Baldwin, please."

1

Early Spring--Hines, Illinois, USA

Catheryn Greye cursed leaving her umbrella in the car as the cold, gray March sky opened up, pelting her with heavy rain. She bolted across the asphalt parking lot of the Veteran's Administration hospital. She held her jean jacket over her head in hopes of warding off the moisture from messing with her long auburn hair. Helluva way to make an impression on her first day.

"Catheryn..."

She came to a dead halt. What was that? She paused to see if she heard it again.

Nothing. A mistaken sound on the breeze? Misinterpreted street noise? It was not at all unusual for the Dead to know she was coming before she arrived at a location. And, if there ever was a location for the Dead to be found...

She entered the sliding doors and paused just inside the entrance, dropping her jean jacket to give it a vigorous shake on the red industrial-pile rug before passing through the second set of sliding doors into the lobby. She side-stepped an orderly pushing a wheelchair-bound patient toward the carport. Examining the rain damage to her mint-colored silk collar shirt, she was grateful to find it minimal.

It was at that moment that a little girl, no more than six years of age, darted through the sliding doors from the hospital side. She had rusty red shoulder-length straight hair, and her tiny body was wearing nothing but a white hospital gown speckled with little flowers. As the freckled, cherub face smiled up at her with an incomplete set of front teeth, a startled Catheryn glanced up through the entrance at the information desk. Not a single administrator, clerk or nurse seemed at all disturbed in their duties due to the actions of the wayward child.

As the door slid closed, it was then that it occurred to the therapist; there was no reason for a child to be treated at a V.A hospital. Not one from the world of the Living, anyway.

The girl glanced over her shoulder to observe what Catheryn was looking at before turning her blue-eyed gaze back up to Catheryn's expression of adult disapproval. The child simply giggled, darting back toward the doorway, the glass doors parting in response. Smiling

mischievously, she darted back toward Catheryn again, causing the sliding

doors to trigger once more.

The child was, obviously, having a bit of fun with the device, but as the

doors slid apart, Catheryn felt uncomfortable eyes on her from another

direction. The petite, black female assistant dressed in light blue scrubs,

looked up from her work at the crescent-shaped counter marked

"Information Desk". She drilled the therapist with a look of stern annoyance.

Catheryn's gaze dropped for any sight of the little girl, but the playful child

had vanished.

Folding her jacket over her arm, there was nothing left for Catheryn to

do but mouth an apology to the assistant before entering the lobby. She

fumbled around inside her black leather messenger bag for her wallet.

Flipping it open to her driver's license, she stepped into the space vacated by

the last person being helped.

"Catheryn…"

She paused, mid-step. There was no mistaking it now. The voice was

more adamant. Male. Her eyes scanned the bustling lobby. No one seemed to

be acknowledging her presence, so she continued on toward the counter. She

simply shook her head. Hospitals…

The clinical therapist placed her identification on the white Formica surface. The assistant's head was back down, absorbed in the paperwork of the last visitor. The woman finally looked up; expectancy edged with a little impatience.

Catheryn slid her credentials forward. "Dr. Catheryn Greye."

The assistant picked up the wallet and examined the identification. Placing it back on the counter, she reached behind her and clipped a stack of papers to the clipboard. Sliding it across the space between them, she slapped a pen and a visitor's badge on top of it.

"Sign here, please," she directed, before returning to her previous task.

And so much for the warm welcome. Catheryn bit her lip nervously as she quickly signed off on the paper and handed the clipboard back. Receiving no further acknowledgement, the young therapist sighed, rounding the station and heading down the hall toward Dr. Steuben's office.

Steuben was an old classmate of her clinical office partner, Dr. David Faustus. He and David still played handball every now and again, so when Catheryn expressed an interest in fulfilling some of her vacant schedule hours down at the V.A., David put in a good word for her.

It had been six months since their return from their exploits at the Bramden House, and try as she might, she just couldn't seem to get back into a regular work rhythm. It wasn't as if she wasn't holding up her end of the practice. Her partner just felt that a change of scene might just be what was needed to find that rhythm again.

She didn't pretend not to know what that meant. She had been rather melancholy since returning from that case and it concerned him, greatly. She wasn't sleeping well either. First it was the nightmares. They ramped up her anxiety; the fear that something horrible was trying to reach across through the veil of sleep to snatch at her, again. But, using her lucid dreaming practices, she was able to ascertain it was nothing but mild post-traumatic stress from their adventures at the house.

Then, there was the other dreams. Dreams that were not so easy to explain away. The whispers. The warmth of a voice that had stirred the very depths of her soul. A warmth that would grow in her heart and spread throughout her body until she awoke in tears. She attempted to manipulate her dreams for more; to determine where exactly Captain Charlie Danforth had gone, and why he was so far away. To speak to him, instead of accepting the infrequent whispers he would share with her. But an impenetrable wall always seemed to block her. It was torture.

Taking advantage of his prescription pad, David had written her a few scripts to help but to no avail. She didn't like prescription sleep aids any more than anti-anxiety or anti-depression meds. There was a side effect to the serotonin reuptake inhibitor that she did not like—it messed with her psychic side. Her extrasensory information did not flow as freely and her mediumistic ability seemed almost muted. Although the sleep aids didn't mess with her intuitive abilities like the other medications, there was just something that bothered her about not being completely aware of her surroundings. The meds were completely fine for other people, and she recommended them to clients herself, but to one who knew what lay in wait in the world just on the other side of the Veil, there was a strong need to have her wits about her at all times.

But she knew if she didn't shake these doldrums soon, the last option was going to be the amber-colored prescription bottle in her medicine cabinet she so desperately wanted to avoid.

And especially now, she didn't want her abilities messed with. Ever since that night of answering the knocking door, her unique ability seemed to expand. It was almost as if the physical action itself opened up something else. She was no longer limited to speaking to the Dead that were lost on this plane of existence; the Dead were now able to reach out to her, from the Other Side.

Everyone, but with the one she so desperately wanted to hear from.

As her thoughts came back to the rather stoic looking older man on the other side of the mahogany desk, she had a strong impression anything even slightly out of the ordinary would be unwelcome here.

Mark Steuben finished scribbling some notes on his desktop-sized calendar as Catheryn took a seat. Immediately, she could tell this man did not appreciate computers and liked the tactile feel of paper. His hair was a thick and generous gray but neatly cut and swept to one side. A button-down blue Oxford shirt and maroon tie peaked out from underneath his white lab coat. A full ruddy face hid behind a pair of silver-rimmed multi-focal glasses. His blue eyes looked up over them to regard the younger therapist with a measured gaze that made Catheryn feel like a specimen on a prepared microscope slide.

"So, you've worked with Dr. Faustus for quite a while now," he observed, candidly. "Is he beginning to bore you?"

Catheryn smiled, bemusedly. "No, not at all. I just expressed an interest in working with the military after a…recent experience. After a few month's introspection, with David's support, I felt there was a skillset there that I could develop and help others at the same time."

"You come from a military background then?"

Catheryn found herself nervously fidgeting with the badge in her lap.

"Well, no, I—"

"—and Dr. Faustus says you are…single?"

"Well, I don't see how that—"

"We have a fair share of female therapists that come down to test the waters—feeling that their *feminine* brand of sensitivity will serve them here," he interjected, firmly. "Make no mistake, Dr. Greye. The brutality that these men and women have faced is nothing like you may have experienced with your patients down at County. Regardless how the field thinks about this, not all trauma is equal. Even your *male* counterparts struggle down here. Burn out tends to be high."

Catheryn felt her jaw tighten, the chauvinistic attitude sending her skin crawling.

He pulled some paperwork from a pile next to him and rapped it on the desktop to align it neatly. Order, she observed, as he placed the pile neatly before him. Above all things, it was about order with him.

And everything in its proper place.

"I have no doubt you think I'm gauging you unfairly, but you have to understand something; these men and women are transitioning from a very violent warzone back into civilian life. They are going to need someone who *understands* that."

She breathed in as she recalled the time back at the house, when she had chosen an inopportune moment to reach in to the memories of a very affected Captain Danforth. She recalled the dirt and smoke, the shaking of the ground. The cries of anguish. It was almost as if she was living it, herself. She released that breath, forcing down the impulse to openly shudder at the memory.

"I feel as if I have a unique perspective on that, sir."

"Relax, Dr. Greye," Steuben continued, his blue eyes continuing to regard her over top of his silver frames. "David wouldn't recommend you for this if he didn't think you could handle it."

The man sighed, setting the neatly-arranged paperwork on the other side of his desk.

"We'll have you here on a probation-measured capacity. It's no different than we treat any other newcomer here," he explained curtly, folding his hands on top of his desk blotter, his stern gaze, unwavering. "Not everyone is cut out for this."

"I understand," Catheryn replied, her green eyes meeting his gaze, unflinchingly. "Completely."

Catheryn folded the coat over her arm and hugged the article to her chest as she took a lap around the building to absorb what had just happened. Despite Steuben's triggering gender-bias and underlying old-school misogyny, he was right in that she had no military experience. It would, undoubtedly, be the first question—and barrier—her clients would put before her. She couldn't be an obstacle to that help. Perhaps she was jumping at the opportunity—any opportunity—to feel close to Charlie Danforth. To help others in a way that he couldn't have been helped, she could attempt to honor his memory. This just…wasn't it.

Catheryn hadn't even realized how long she had been walking when the voice of an elderly woman broke through her thoughts. Her pale green eyes were drawn up the taupe-painted corridor up toward her left. The nurse's station to her right appeared vacant. Since the older woman's voice seemed somewhat distressed, she weighed the appropriateness of entering the room. Steuben had accepted her, even if under probation, so the privacy policy shouldn't be a barrier.

Catheryn knocked on the door frame before entering the room. It was at that point she noted the conversation, abruptly, stopped.

An elderly African-American woman lay in the bed. Her short, curly-gray hair had been freshly-combed; her frail form wrapped in a comfortable white robe. Her dark skin peaked out from beneath the plush folds of the garment, her arms and face speckled with a generous number of age spots giving away her advanced years. At the end of her bed stood a lean African-American gentleman. His hair was not as gray as the bed-occupant, but his aged complexion was not dissimilar. The patient looked up at the new arrival, her watery brown eyes looking surprised at her sudden appearance. Unlike the startled woman, the gentleman visitor didn't seem the slightest bit affected, gazing up at Catheryn with a warm, welcoming smile.

"Oh, are you a doctor? Oh, please!" pleaded the elderly woman. "I know it's after visiting hours, but please don't send Daniel away. He tries to come when the nursing staff is here, but they are always in a rush. Why…they seem to run right through him as though he's not even there."

Catheryn's attention was drawn back to the male visitor, who now appeared to be chuckling quietly to himself. The good humor in the man's dark eyes were all Catheryn needed to understand just why the nurses' attentions may have seemed that way.

As solid—as present—as the man looked, Daniel was not of the Living.

"Oh, I'm not looking to run anyone out," the young therapist explained warmly, placing a comforting hand on the patient's shoulder. "I just heard your voice, and since the nurses were away, I thought I might check and see if you needed something."

"Very kind. It is a little difficult to get attention sometimes," the older woman sighed, giving Catheryn's hand a good-natured pat. "Abigale Freemont. A pleasure to meet you."

"You can call me Catheryn." The therapist smiled wistfully. "I knew an 'Abigale' once. She was from a…difficult time. She was a real force to be reckoned with."

"So is mine," the gentleman said, his doting gaze falling upon the frail patient.

"I'm sure we would have gotten along," Abigale Freemont responded, her chin raising a fraction, and for a moment, some of that frailty seemed to vanish. "I was a nurse in a triage camp during Korea. It's where I met my Daniel."

Her dark eyes were drawn back to the comforting gaze of her companion at the other end of the bed.

"Even though fraternizing with the patients was strictly forbidden…it was love at first sight."

Catheryn drew back to hug the coat to her body. "I'm sure they understood some things just…can't be helped."

Abigale Freemont struggled to ease up from her prone position in the bed. "We were just about to leave for the Officer's Club for dinner. Would you like to join us?"

Catheryn startled, uncertain whether to attempt to dissuade the patient from moving, or to call a nurse. "Oh, I—"

"There's a real swingin' band playin' tonight," the older woman poked persuadingly.

"My Abigale sure can cut a rug," Daniel muttered, his eyes sparkling mischievously. "But, I'm sure the doctor here is needed elsewhere, baby."

The elderly patient smiled warmly up at Catheryn. "Another time, perhaps."

Catheryn was about to respond when she started at the claxon sound of an alarm coming from behind her. It was coming from the nurses' station. An echo of the same alarm blared from inside the room, a fraction of a second later. She managed to back out of the doorway just as two nurses materialized from nowhere, bursting in to the room. As Catheryn observed the invading party, she noted the frail Abigale had succumbed to the embrace of her pillow. The discombobulating noise and activity sent the doctor's mind reeling, sending her to scurry out of the way of the male attendant rushing in with a crash cart. As the therapist backed away, she heard the senior nurse begin to bark orders. It was in that heightened state of alertness that Catheryn caught a movement out of the corner of her eye.

The young doctor could make out a couple dressed in olive drab, strolling casually down the hallway. Their calm demeanor was so completely contrary to the chaos in the hospital room that it couldn't help but attract her attention. Military uniforms in a V.A. hospital were not unheard of, but the gentleman's neatly-pressed slacks and dress shirt, and the woman's matching skirt just below the knee, spoke of an earlier fashion. The cut of the woman's well-tailored brown wool blazer flared away from her tiny waist; her hair pinned up in a beautiful wave of ebony. She looked perfect for an evening out. The uniformed woman flung a smile toward Catheryn from over her shoulder.

There was no mistaking the woman in the hospital room was the same smiling back at the therapist—give or take about sixty years. Abigale was quite a looker in her day. It was no wonder Daniel was charmed. It was clear that the two were not turning back, and their exit from the world of the Living, was a permanent one.

The therapist's attention was drawn back to the din in the room before her. She hated that the emergency staff were expending such energy on a cause already lost, but what exactly would she tell them? She decided to take the couple's lead and find her way out of the establishment.

2

"Catheryn..."

The young therapist found herself fighting through the white gauze of her ethereal surroundings, trying to find the source of the soft male voice murmuring her name.

"Catheryn..."

Where was she? The last thing she remembered was leaving the hospital, and...and...

She raised her hands as if that would have some effect on the haze before her, but as she did so, her hands found purchase on something. Wool. Blue wool.

Her pale green eyes rose to lock with the familiar dark, mysterious eyes beneath thick brooding eyebrows. But the eyes were far from brooding. They regarded her with soft affection. She felt his rough, calloused hand touch her cheek, but with that contact came an ecstatic jolt of energy that ran like lightning through her body.

"Catheryn, stop looking behind you," his warm low voice coaxed. *"Your future is not behind you. Everything is as it should be. See what is in front of you."*

She closed her eyes. She didn't want to hear him. She wanted to *feel* him; the warmth of his presence that seemed to surround her like a welcome embrace. She leaned in to that feeling. She missed it. Missed him.

"You must...see..."

The screech of tires and Doppler effect of the angry car horn rudely jolted Catheryn from her pleasant void. She had been very sleep-deprived the last few days, but she hadn't realized how much until now. She had to be completely exhausted to drift off to sleep in a metro cab.

"Suicides aren't scheduled until Monday, you jack wagon!" the salty middle-aged cabbie exclaimed out the window.

Glancing in the rear-view mirror at his passenger, his expression shifted to one of apology.

"Sorry, about that," he muttered, yanking the wheel over. "Tourists!"

The cab pulled off to the west side by the intersection and let Catheryn out. She scurried out into the rain, her denim coat still over her head as she darted to the steps leading up into the office building that housed their clinical practice offices. She dropped her denim jacket from over her head as she passed under the security of the door overhang but paused before the doors. In her haste to escape the rain she had almost tripped over Mr. Daulton. The longtime hotdog vendor was a favorite of the office. He was there; stooped over his hotdog card, sporting his usual white apron tied about his neck. His Cubs ballcap was mashed down over gray hair that always seemed in need of a trim. With the early afternoon rain, his multicolored umbrella over his cart looked even more inviting. Besides, Catheryn and Dr. Faustus were very good customers; enough so that Mr. Daulton could recall their "usual" by memory. Of course, how many *other* people ordered jalapenos on their Chicago special? Perhaps she could repay her partner's wrangling of her morning schedule with a little lunch.

"Catheryn!"

She was so used to the other, more subtle voices trying to get her attention that the voice from the Living world shook her. She turned, the broad smile of perfect white veneers announcing themselves before the rest of the man. Even though the pomade in his blondish hair was a bit overcome by the afternoon rain, all five-foot six inches of Andrew Baldwin still looked his million-dollar best in his tan designer trench, gray trousers and black, highly-shined dress shoes. Before she could stop him, the realtor nearly toppled her in an enthusiastic embrace.

"It's been an age!" he laughed, the sincerity of a smile finally registering in his hazel eyes.

Catheryn couldn't help but return his infectious smile. She dropped the denim jacket from over her head as they moved under the protective overhang of the front door way.

"Andrew," she chuckled, incredulously. "What brings you about to our neighborhood?"

"That brownstone down on Addison," he beamed proudly. "Finally sold it!"

"Finally? That's been on the market for…awhile, hasn't it?"

She'd walked past it often enough. Its peculiar *character* was hard to miss. She lost count how many times the paranormally-active address would set her psychic sense ablaze along her scalp as she walked by it. It would make sense that, of all people, Andrew Baldwin would attack the sale of that particular asset with his unique psychic skillset.

He leaned in, dropping his tone to something more conspiring. "That one—took some time to clear!"

As she tilted her head in conversational interest, she caught something over Andrew's left shoulder. A young, waifish woman was watching the conversation between them, intently, with her large dark eyes. She wore her dark hair in a very stylish bob common in the 1920s. Her skin was of fine porcelain and her large lips a rouge red. The most peculiar thing about her was, even though everyone around her was scurrying madly to get out of the rain, her hair and makeup remained pristine, as was her black silk sheath dress.

It was upon that very realization that the woman's eyes darted to fix on Catheryn's, one corner of her red painted lips curling up in a sly smile. Yes, the woman wasn't really there. Not to the average person, anyway.

Within a blink, she was intimately close at Andrew's shoulder, her dark gaze sweeping over the realtor's form in a way that most would consider provocative. It was enough for Catheryn to consider interrupting her acquaintance.

Instead, she simply said, with one eye on the specter. "I won't tell anyone."

"It's alright. The place is completely cleared out now," Baldwin declared, smugly, completely unaware of the presence hovering at his side. "Sold in two weeks. Made a nice profit, too. Client hasn't reported a single problem. We should go out to dinner to celebrate."

The ethereal woman's demure expression soured in an instant, her haughty gaze turning on Catheryn.

"Oh…oh, my schedule is pretty tight over the next few days," the young therapist stammered, trying to keep her eyes from meeting the gaze of the disdainful specter. "Raincheck?"

Andrew flashed her his usual realtor-of-the-year grin. "Sure! Sure. Another time. My treat, okay?"

He turned to head out from under the overhang when he pivoted back to her, abruptly. "Oh, and I completely forgot to tell you. The whole reason for me stopping over here—Bramden House is for sale. Again."

Catheryn was shocked. "What?! What happened to Peter?"

"Turned out it was not what he thought it was," Andrew smiled, knowingly, shrugging his shoulders. "Too…quiet, I suppose?"

Considering their tumultuous past, she admitted there was no love lost for Peter Elgin. But, for the enthusiastic ghost hunter whose whole persona came from cultivating haunted properties for commercial use, to just…give up?

Andrew shook his head, throwing up his hands to ward off that conversation.

"Not my listing; not my problem. You couldn't pay me *enough* to go through that again!"

He turned, casting a hand up in the damp spring air to hail a cab. Yes;

Andrew may have been using his special abilities for his own personal gain, but he had learned his lesson. The therapist's aventurine green eyes couldn't help but steal a look at the obsessed entity that continued to follow at his elbow.

Well, perhaps, he would. Eventually. But Catheryn had to admit; his news came as a surprise that stirred up old anxieties. She turned back to Mr. Daulton who was just completing the order for two more customers. The middle-aged vendor's brown eyes caught hers, and smiled.

"Would that be the 'usual', Dr. Greye," the man offered in his familiar jovial Chicago manner.

"Of course," she answered. "The special. Make it two."

Catheryn sat at her desk, wrapped in the cozy, mint-colored cardigan she kept on her office chair. She stirred a spoon, absentmindedly, in the cup of coffee that was before her. Her mind was nowhere near the caffeinated beverage.

Bramden House. For sale. She couldn't get over it. The house was empty once more.

Wasn't it?

Her eyes lingered over the plastic black eight-ball toy on the right-hand corner of her desk. Nope. Her professional partner was right; it was a piece of superstitious nonsense; a piece of plastic. Beneath her notice and an insult to her skills as a psychic. She might as well chuck it in to the garbage.

She grabbed it, but once the oracle was in the palm of her right hand, the compulsion seized her. The therapist brought it back to her chest, vigorously shaking the object with both hands. Closing her eyes, she took a deep, cleansing breath; was Bramden House occupied by spirit?

She felt the reluctance to look. Ridiculous. When it came to learning about the things she feared most, her approach was always to rip the metaphorical bandage off. She briskly flipped the black sphere over.

Yes

The shock caused her to slam the flattened surface of the plastic toy on to the desktop, so much so that she feared breakage of the viewing window. It would be an awkward conversation explaining how the leaking blue dye ended up all over her client files.

David Faustus happened by the desk at that instant; a manila folder tucked under one arm, ready for filing. His salt-and-pepper hair was hastily combed back, his jaw line dusted with white stubble. With his choice of blue Oxford collar shirt and argyle vest, he appeared more like a professor late for class than a doctor seeing patients. Any other day, she would have likely called him out on it, but not today.

Her senior partner was more attentive, stopping just short of her desk.

"What's with you?" Faustus asked, eyebrows pricked inquisitively.

She gauged in the back of her mind if the whole thing warranted bringing up, and then, thought the better of it.

"Nothing," she muttered, innocently, stealthily sliding the ball in to her side desk drawer. "What's on the docket today?"

He pivoted, the manila folder in his hand coming to rest upon her desk. "Funny you should ask. I have another possible candidate to test for the triple blind study. Wondered if you could do it."

"Me? Why not you?"

"How do you think this one ended up on the list?" He smiled his wry, disarming smile. "Could use a second opinion."

"I thought you promised only to use that superpower for good," she said, smirking at the mild manipulation. "Save it for someone that it will work on. I'll do it."

As he walked away, she did a cursory check of her left drawer for blue dye damage. Satisfied that the paper contents were safe, she rose from her seat.

DARCIE McGRATH

3

Catheryn was excited about the ability to form the mediumship study. The grant award was a surprise. There were a handful of research groups testing mediums' psychic abilities using the triple blind method, so it was exciting that a fledgling operation like theirs was even considered for the grant. Needless to say, Faustus was doing his utmost to make sure the data collected was spotless.

She stuck her head in to the administrative offices to look for the assistant.

"Amelia, is the subject in the reading room?"

The young twenty-something student had a head of unruly brown curls clipped back from a face that was a pasty white; screaming less exposure to sun than Catheryn had, herself. The intern's dark rimmed glasses set off her bookish appearance, as did the manila envelope pressed to her ample bosom. She was not a small woman at five foot, eight inches tall, but in Catheryn's presence, she always appeared somewhat timid. She had joined Catheryn and

David's research team from the university here in Chicago. At twenty-four, she was seeking her masters in Psychology, but she also had a strong interest in human consciousness studies and desperate to prove her worth. Wanting to put her analytics classes to work, she joined them for her Spring semester to assist in data analysis in hopes of adding a live parapsychology research project to her résumé.

"Yes, Dr. Greye. The subject has been set up in the reading room per your instructions," she said softly, but confidently.

"Has she done any questionnaires, yet?"

The young intern pulled a clipboard out from behind the manila envelope.

"Yes," the assistant replied. "Dr. Faustus sent out his questionnaires last week."

"Good. Be sure he sends any supplementals after we're done," the therapist stated. "Note this is not for score. This is a test run only."

The young woman looked up at her from over the clipboard, somewhat reluctantly. "You're going to test the subject yourself, Doctor?"

"Randomizing the sitter is part of the blind study. It's okay," the young therapist stated, shrugging off her cardigan sweater and draping it on the brown pleather couch in the observation room. "You can just run the

Lottery for another sitter tomorrow."

The lab had a computer that randomized a volunteer to be paired with the medium in order to be scheduled for a lab reading. This kept the volunteers, scorers, and researchers distanced from researcher bias in the experiment. They called the computer program the Lottery.

Catheryn waited patiently on the other side of the observational two-way mirror, as Amelia entered the room with the large three-panel room divider. The young woman readjusted the empty office chair and disappeared behind the panels. When Amelia re-emerged, she was absent the manila envelope but still clutching the clipboard to her chest. She glanced up in Catheryn's direction, her large brown eyes darting, self-conscious to the fact she was being watched through the glass. It was a natural response. As Catheryn watched, the intern glanced behind. Amelia turned back to the mirrored glass and nodded, signifying readiness.

Catheryn could have chosen to do the reading from the comfort of the observation room. The intercom switch was right below the glass. The microphone above the medium would have been piped in to where she was standing, but she wanted to be closer. She wanted to be in the "sitter" chair for once. It could be the last time since they were moving away to in-person testing and going to phone readings-only.

She peered through the small rectangular safety glass before turning the spherical metal knob of the faux wood paneled door of the reading room. She entered the room and let the hydraulic catch close the door quietly. The tall brown, three-paneled room divider was large enough to keep the test medium from seeing Catheryn, and just as much so Catheryn couldn't see her. It was best that the medium—or the "reader"—to have little contact, or impressions, of the test subject they were about to read. The report would assign Catheryn a tracking number, labeling her as the "sitter"—the subject being read.

The room around them was not very inspiring. The taupe-painted walls were bare; nothing to distract or indirectly influence the mediumistic impressions of the reading. The lights overhead were the flat, rectangular LED insets. They stared, unblinkingly, back at her from the white-tiled ceiling as she made her way to the singular, orange plastic chair next to the divider. It reminded her of the small chairs from elementary school with the four brushed-steel legs and slightly molded seat. As she sat on the uncomfortable plastic, she made a mental note that if they restarted in-person readings, *maybe* they could afford something just a little more comfortable for sitters in the future.

The intercom crackled to life, and the hollow voice of Amelia filled the space. The formalities were few; the assistant read the usual disclaimer about the reading being recorded.

"You may begin," the assistant concluded, the microphone closing off with an audible *click*.

Catheryn took in a deep breath and let it out, vaguely aware of noises coming from over the divider. It sounded like the shuffling of paper and a pen scribbling away. It didn't surprise her. She'd seen other psychics use pen to paper as a form of meditation; a free flow of energy to get themselves into the zone.

"It's important to discuss how I receive impressions," the test subject started. "I often receive images, colors, words, and sometimes music. Occasionally, I'll receive letters and numbers. It's important to note these as they may not make sense at the time but may make sense to you later."

Catheryn didn't bring paper. It was irrelevant in observing how the test subject worked. It was rare that she received anything of substance from such exercises anyway.

"I may ask you 'yes' or 'no' questions to validate the reading is heading in the right direction, and to the right receiver. Does this make sense?"

"Yes."

"Who comes through is not necessarily controllable, but the sooner we make a validated connection, it is possible for more to make contact during the course of the reading. Do you understand?"

"Yes."

The speaking went on pause, the only sound from over the divider the continued scribbling of pen to paper by the test reader.

"There is a Caucasian, middle-aged male coming through. Slender build. Blonde...no...strawberry blonde. He's making that distinction as if it's important. Does this make sense to you?"

Catheryn picked at a strand of her long auburn hair and twisted it around her finger, a pang of emotion causing her heart to ache. Regardless, the therapist did her best to keep all emotion out of her voice.

"Yes."

"He's wearing a pastel-colored plaid shirt," the medium continued. "He has a full moustache and he's wearing wire-rimmed glasses. He's indicating a sharp pain in his chest. Not from an impact, but his passing was quick...one, two, three...gone. Does that make sense?"

Her father. It was undoubtedly, her father. He always annoyed her mother by wearing the most garish plaid shirts which he, inevitably ruined, doing odd jobs around the house. He had died when Catheryn was in grad school. Massive heart attack. As impressive as the information was, she still kept her voice monotone.

"Yes," she whispered.

"He has an interesting small black figurine in his hand. It's a chess piece…yes. It appears to be a knight. Does this make sense to you?"

Catheryn made sure her breathing was regulated before she answered. A slight change in vocal inflection from the sitter—even a change in breathing pattern—could form as a readable 'tell' by those readers who could be attempting a practice known as "cold reading". A skilled 'cold reader' could easily mimic a mediumistic reading by reading body language, augmented by observation of outward sitter appearance—clothing, hairstyle, jewelry, etcetera. It was why a physical divider was maintained between the sitter and reader.

But the number of validations the medium was coming through with were stretching far beyond chance odds. Regardless, she wanted to do her best not to tip her hand to the test reader.

"Yes."

"He's handing the chess piece to someone else now. There's an older gentleman coming through who is a little taller, but heavier around the middle. He has thinning gray hair and is beaming at you, proudly. If I didn't know any better, I would have suggested him as a father figure to you, but there's an obvious father-son…father-son…connection between the two here. Does this make sense?"

The young therapist closed her eyes and took an unsteady breath. Control. She had to control herself. She needed to keep any emotion out of her voice. Her grandfather. Of course, he would come through. So many questions she wanted to ask him. Where had he gone? Why did she not see him anymore? He had been there to walk her through her gifts at the beginning of her life, and now…Now, with her gift changing, she needed him now more than ever.

The medium didn't ask for permission to continue this time.

"He's showing me the chess piece again. He's asking if you still play. Wait a minute. There's something…someone…" The medium's tone seemed to change abruptly, bordering on the defensive. "You don't understand. You don't understand how this works. You are going to have to wait your turn!"

The urgent tone of the medium snapped Catheryn free of her nostalgia as she listened with alarmed attention.

"You are crossing the line. You must wait!" The medium's voice sounded strained. "I…I can't! Too much! Back *off*! It's male. He's very strong. He's asserting his dominance. He's demanding to be heard the way *he* wants to be heard."

The scribbling sounds from the other side of the divider seemed to intensify. Catheryn could almost perceive the writing utensil carving its way through the paper.

"No! That's…no!" the medium objected, her voice disrupted. "That's not permitted. You may *not*…you may NOT!"

The scribbling came to an immediate halt. The silence was nearly deafening. Catheryn was on the verge of rising from her plastic seat, ready to call the session completed when she heard the medium expel a forced breath, breaking the silence. The therapist relaxed in to her seat, once more, as the inhale/exhale pattern repeated for a few more seconds. Catheryn recognized the practice as something she had done as a medium, herself. The reader was attempting to ground her own personal energy.

"I'm sorry," the female voice offered weakly from over the divider. "He tried to jump me. That's not allowed. It's rare for that to happen, but I had to break the connection. I'm very sorry."

Catheryn wished at that moment to see the medium's face. She had spirits try to jump into *her*, taking advantage of *her* body, *her* feelings. It was an invasion of the most sacred trust and a reminder of just how vulnerable mediums were in that open state.

And it was at that moment that she realized her personal conflict of interest in testing these mediums. This medium would be her last.

Amelia's voice over the intercom brought the therapist back to task.

"Okay, I believe we can call this session," the assistant announced. "Thank you for your time, Number Twelve. If you exit out the side door, we'd like to perform an exit interview. If the sitter would remain seated, please."

The conclusion of the reading left Catheryn unsettled. Who—or what—was that? It was so forceful. Was the uninvited arrival something personal attached to the research medium, or was it something personal for Catheryn? Maybe the test subject was not a good fit for the project, after all.

She waited for the audible click of the closing door. The test subject was gone. Catheryn wasn't supposed to go into the reading side of the room until the assistant had cleared it. If there was anything worth sharing, it would come up in the data analysis meeting. But no; she had to look. She had to see.

She squeezed by the divider to enter the test subject area. In the center of that section of room was a chair with an extended right flat arm surface for taking notes. Strewn about the gray industrial-style carpeting were pages and pages of writing paper. Many were covered with indecipherable scribbles and swirls in black, ball-point ink. Nothing there of consequence. The remaining pad of paper was her target. Catheryn's breathing quickened as she rounded the chair. On the pad, scratched in strong, deliberate strokes, were clear letters. All capital letters. Her fingers ran over the page, her pale green eyes wide in disbelief as she took in the message so blatantly carved there.

I AM HERE

4

The ghostly light of the late, dreary afternoon painted long shadows in the living room of Catheryn's apartment. She had changed out of her work clothes and in to her signature gray yoga pants, and chose her black t-shirt emblazoned with the logo of her favorite Irish pub. She had even poured herself a cup of chamomile tea in hopes of calming down from the strangeness of the day. It wasn't working. She anxiously paced before the large picture window, not even sparing a look at the urban sprawl below. Her long auburn hair, pulled back in a scrunchie, flicked back and forth like the tail of an agitated cat as she moved.

For a moment, she paused, her lithe figure in stark silhouette before the window as she turned to address the far wall.

"It was just so…unsettling," she said, her hands clenching and unclenching. "First, the cab ride, and…and the lab. I was being watched. Observed. And the medium—what was that? It was so intrusive, so invasive.

It felt like some sort of an attack. I don't know who or what it was. It was so…forceful!"

For anyone else, it would have been disturbing, and even frightening, to see the unusually tall figure detach itself from the shadowy corner of the room. The garish light of the day made the gaunt porcelain skin of the visitor's face even more ghastly. His high cheekbones and angular features only looked more severe in the sparse light, but his magnificent blue-green eyes still managed to maintain their usual unearthly glow. Anyone else appearing that way may have unnerved her, but she was quite familiar with her spiritual guide, Ralph, and his ethereal comings and goings in her apartment.

And, at that moment, she was in great need of his advice.

The ethereal being arched an intrigued eyebrow in her direction. "And just how do you think the medium felt?"

She sighed in mild agitation. There were times his inquiries made her feel like an admonished child.

"David thoroughly vets them for any issues when they complete their testing session," Catheryn countered, nonetheless taking her tone down a notch. "As the sitter, I'm not meant to know. But still…who *was* that?"

He exhaled loudly through his nose, his lips remaining a thin line, his jaw set as his gaze sternly regarded a spot on the floor. The shift in his demeanor caused her to freeze as she fixed him with an intense stare.

"You know something. What are you not telling me?"

"He was warned not to interfere," he said with a tone that was both quiet and firm, his gaze still avoiding hers. "He was given strict instructions…"

Her aventurine green eyes grew wide, shock mixed with betrayal flickering across her features. He didn't need to mention the name. It was all becoming too clear. Everything from the hospital, to the car ride, to the lab. It had all been Captain Charles Danforth.

Charlie.

For months, Catheryn had heard nothing; not even a whisper from the man that had been the most intense, most personal relationship she had ever had in her life thus far. A connection she had found with no other. So, the spectral soldier from the American Civil War wasn't exactly *alive*, but in her unique experience, with her unique talents, did that really matter? Her fingers skimmed over the center of her chest, the faint memory of a feeling so emotionally charged, so ecstatically powerful, threatening to flood her with emotion.

And Ralph was, intentionally, keeping him from her; knowing full well the incredible impact he had had on her lonely and isolated existence.

"Why?" she stammered. "Why…why would you—"

He met her gaze, and to Catheryn's surprise, she saw regret there.

"I should have stopped it," the guide whispered, his gaze falling to the floor. "I never should have allowed that to happen. I should have stopped it before it even began."

"'Stop it'?" Catheryn was puzzled, searching for his eyes. "Stop what?"

"I should have stopped it the moment I realized…" The guide shook his head in agitation. "…the moment I realized that this wasn't just a…a…curiosity."

"You're acting as if it was some cataclysm. Some…plague—"

"No," Ralph bit out. "It was worse."

All Catheryn could do was blink at him, incredulous.

He fixed her with the most serious gaze that she had ever seen him give.

"Do you question the eternity of the soul's existence?"

She reflected on the last several decades of her life; her work as a medium only of a few encounters. "Of course."

"Why is it, do you suppose, that you do not recall the life before?"

She paused. A few thoughts floated to mind, but she could not land on a singular answer. But she had no doubt who had one.

"To move forward. To move on with the task and the lesson, at hand," he responded, firmly. "The lessons and tasks you agreed to learn. Looking back only discourages that."

"He loves you with a fierce intensity you will never again feel on this earth. You will measure all relationships after this and always find them wanting. Always." His intense blue-green eyes shifted away from hers, filled with regret. "You'll pass on other opportunities, other chances to make connections out of some sense of loyalty, but the memory of what you had will fade. Over time, you will forget. You'll fight it. You may deny it. You won't want to, but you will."

Catheryn felt some of the earlier counseling training floating to the forefront of her memory.

"You're talking about the Stages of Grief," Catheryn snorted.

"It is," he replied. "You very well know it is. Some on the other side are just as challenged by the stages of grief as the Living are, with one minor difference. For you, time will cause the pain to fade; the trials and tribulations of living will provide the distraction for us to move forward. The feeling of loss will lessen in its intensity…"

The seriousness of his blue-green eyes never left hers.

"He needs to leave you in peace. Allow you to live your life. *This* life."

Catheryn found her eyes brimming with tears. She angrily swiped at them as they threatened to spill down her cheeks.

"'Peace'? I would not consider what I have been going through the last several months as 'peace'!" she stammered, turning toward her hall closet.

Ralph stepped between her in the wall, drilling his gaze in to her own.

"Precisely. You have to *choose* to let him go," he said, with his unshakable calm voice. "I know he's been trying to get you to do just that. Release him."

Catheryn's hands went to the sides of her head, as if trying to shut his voice out, her own philosophical words of ripping the bandage off, resonating in her head. She reached forward and brusquely, threw the closet door open, claiming her purple roller travel bag.

"Where are you going?" the ethereal being muttered, exasperatedly as she tossed the suitcase on the bed. "Catheryn—"

"I need to go down and talk to him."

"There's no need for you to go down there," he protested, trying to draw her ardent attention away from packing. "Locality is nothing to him. He is not there. You know that."

"I can't reach him here!" She wheeled around on him, her ponytail flinging over her shoulder, revealing tears streaming down her face. "For the first time in my life I can reach both sides of the Veil, but I can't reach *him*. If

I have to do it, I have to do it *my way*. It was there it began. It's there it will end."

Ralph drew back, startled at her defiance, as she pulled out the telescoping handle of her roller travel bag and dragging it down the hall to her bedroom. Ralph had to *blink* his ethereal form to meet her there.

Ralph took a measured breath, as she threw her case on the bed and unzipped it, gathering items from nearby drawers.

The guide spoke with carefully-crafted tonality. "You don't have to go there."

His quietude nearly grew her ire, and she turned on him.

"He said it himself: "I AM HERE"—why would he give that message if he didn't mean for me to find him?" She looked in to his eyes; those beautiful blue-green eyes, unflinchingly. "He *needs* to speak to me. And I need to speak to him."

The look on the face of her ethereal teacher was if she had struck him. She had never countermanded him so directly. Not since the battle at the house.

He could only watch, in stunned silence, as she wheeled down the hallway, case in hand. The shock began to melt into sorrow as she gathered her purse and keys from the breakfast nook. She had every right to make her own decisions, which mostly followed his well-informed advice, but not now, when it was possibly the most pivotal moment to do so.

And he knew, just as well, he was not permitted to stop her.

As the front door closed behind her, only he truly knew where that would lead, and it shook him to his very core, filling him with dread.

5

Regional Airport, Burlington, Iowa, USA

Catheryn easily found a seat on a flight into Burlington, Iowa. The quaint little airport had regular commuter flights to and from O'Hare, but the weekend traffic consisted mostly of outgoing tourists to the Windy City, so finding a seat on an inbound flight was not a problem.

Establishing itself in the early 1800's as a river boomtown on the mighty Mississippi, the town of nearly 26,000 people later became more famous for its railroad. It also featured one of the "crookedest streets in the world" according to an article in her travel magazine, but visiting such curiosities would have to be postponed to a later date. Her anxious attention extended far beyond the city limits. And thanks to the intimate size of the airport, she had collected her baggage and was at the head of the rental car line in no time at all. She was just in the middle of pulling her driver's license when the lady at the counter moved a sign over in front of the slot at the window— "Back in Five Minutes."

Catheryn blinked, incredulously, as the woman walked away. "Really?"
she muttered to the empty space in front of her.

The next wave of new arrivals was rushing around her, and she turned
to secure her roller bag.

"I can help you here, ma'am."

She turned to find a young, twenty-something gentleman at the service
window, wearing a navy polo with the airport's insignia. Pinned above it was
a nameplate of burnished gold, etched with the name "Cam". His brown hair
was short and needly brushed to one side, the bright smile on his face
sparking a gleam in his brown eyes.

"Fantastic!" Catheryn muttered, sliding the identification across the
Formica counter top. "Thank you!"

"Can I ask your destination?"

"Bentonsport. Van Buren County."

The young man's face brightened even further. "Oh, best deer hunting
in the state down there. Lots of deer…matter of fact…" The youth leaned
across the counter, conspiringly. "…you might wanna opt for the insurance."

She chuckled, good-naturedly, having travelled often enough to expect
the emphasized pitch to sell extra insurance. "Oh, I'm a cautious driver."

The young man's dark eyes seemed to shift in their intensity, his smile dimming considerably. The sudden shift in the young man's demeanor caused Catheryn to shift back a step.

"You can never be too careful," he stated, flatly.

Before she could react any further, one of the rushed passengers collided with her bag, and Catheryn turned to rein it in closer to her. When she turned back, she blinked in surprise. He was gone.

She leaned across the counter, straining to see down the left and right side of the office aisle. How did he do that? As she turned to look right again, she almost collided with a young African-American woman sporting long intricate braids and the signature bright red polo of the rental car agency.

"I'm sorry, ma'am," the agent smiled, collecting her composure from the intruding presence on her side of the counter. "I'm Tamera. Can I help you?"

Catheryn could only stammer. "I'm sorry. I thought the young man was helping me. Short dark hair, dark eyes…he was just here."

"Oh, I haven't seen him," the young woman replied, leaning back to re-check for anyone in the back hallway. "I can help you, though."

The young therapist reasserted her smile and slid her identification toward the agent. "Catheryn. Greye."

The rental car agent typed away at her computer and turned to collect the keys. The printer whirred away, and once completed, the assistant retrieved the contract forms and placed both articles in the customer contract envelope. She handed them to Catheryn.

"Lot B. Stall 4."

"Thank you."

The young attendant watched the female customer walk away when she turned to find her female co-worker arriving, her blonde head bobbing under the counter to tuck her backpack away.

"Hey, Jess!" the agent greeted, her face scrunching in a quizzical expression as her partner resurfaced above the counter. "You haven't seen Cam back here this morning, have you?"

Jess straightened up, her usual bubbly smile, failing. "Oh, no one…told you."

Her counterpart's vacant blink answered her without words.

"About the car accident last night?" When no recognition appeared on her partner's face, the blonde's smile faded, completely. "Somebody told me it was a deer…"

Neither woman realized the entire exchange was being witnessed by a silent pair across the terminal floor. Not one of the bustling travelers seemed to pay the two any mind as they rushed to their destination. The young man named Cam watched the two girls, his expression grim as the tall, lean gentleman next to him observed the scene along with him.

"I don't know if that helped or not," the young man muttered, looking up in to the magnificent blue-green eyes of his new acquaintance.

The unusually-radiant, yet pale face, gazed down at him with a serene smile. "Of course, you did."

"Well, my young friend," the lean figure muttered to the companion at his side, his blue-green eyes continuing to watch his female charge leave through the sliding terminal doors. "I think it's time we moved on. Don't you? I believe we have some people waiting for you."

The young man named Cam took the gentle hand at the back of his shoulder as the sign to start moving ahead. Once the ethereal being was sure he no longer held the young man's attention, the smile evaporated, his gaze shifting to watch Catheryn walk away. The last of the guide's interference cards were played. The rest would be up to her.

She stood next to the 4-door dark sedan she had rented, fumbling with the keys in the open-air rental car parking lot. She closed her eyes against the light of mid-day, reaching out with her unique senses for anything—or any one—feeling even slightly like the old house.

Nothing. Perhaps she needed to be closer.

After depositing her roller bag in to the trunk and spending almost twenty minutes configuring her cell phone to the Bluetooth system, she plugged in the address of the house in to her phone and was on her way.

As she got underway, she began to regret not driving down before. The instructions the phone gave seemed somewhat confused, and she was pretty sure she had overshot the address. Her suspicions were confirmed when the dilapidated old farmhouse loomed in to view, with the phone stating, "You have reached your destination." Backing out of the driveway, she settled upon a different point of reference, and struck out on the road, again.

Her stomach was growling as she came upon the familiar farm town of Keosauqua, and she managed upon the pizza place Andrew, David, and her had frequented on their final stay. Managing to grab a bite to eat as well as grabbing better directions, she was back on the road by five.

As she managed back on the Highway J-40 turnoff, she began to see the flaw in her strategy. Before she had a place to stay. Now, she did not. Perhaps she could backtrack to the old riverboat hotel back in Keosauqua after she had concluded her business.

If she could find a way to conclude her business.

She was beginning to think that Ralph was right. What was she doing here? No matter how much she strained her senses out ahead of her, nothing felt as if it was connecting with anything remotely familiar. The old riverboat hotel back in Keo had more "presence" than anything in front of her. What if all of this was just a waste of time?

Her thought was cut off as she rounded the bend and saw a shape dart out of the wood. A deer. She slowed down just enough to allow it to clear the road. She would have to be careful. If anything were to happen out here—

The second deer caught her completely unaware, and she hit the brake hard. The combination of the sudden braking movement entering a sharp bend in the road threw the car into a sideways skid. Her heart leapt as the car spun about, catching the opposite gravel shoulder. The sudden traction of the gravel flipped the car over, sending it careening down a wooded embankment where it struck something hard. The last thing Catheryn remembered was the sense of weightlessness before the left side of her head hit something unyielding. After that moment, everything went black.

David Faustus was not a happy man. Steuben had called to follow up with the meeting he had taken that morning with Catheryn, and he had to admit that Catheryn had, yet, to follow up with him about it. When he called Catheryn's cell, it had gone to voicemail. If she was to start her time with the V.A., scheduling plans had to be made, and paperwork needed to be filled out. That, combined with Amelia's report on how the lab session had gone, there was obviously a lengthier conversation to be had.

By the time he had closed up the office, grabbed supper, and returned home, it was well past eight. Retiring to the bedroom, he donned his robe before collapsing in to his favorite armchair next to the bed and attempted to call Catheryn again.

Voicemail.

He sighed through pursed lips, as he put the phone down on the bedside table. That was unusual. It wasn't like Catheryn to not return a missed call and even more unusual to miss two. Flipping on the standing light next to his chair, he reached for his current reading interest from his bedside table. Perhaps he would read a bit while he waited for her to call him back.

It must have been somewhere between Chapters Thirteen and Fourteen that he must have drifted off to sleep, because when he glanced over at the alarm clock on the bedside table, the angry red numbers of 2:45 A.M. glared back at him. He reached over to the phone on the bedside table and checked it for messages.

None.

That did it. Something had to be wrong. He rose from the armchair to find the number to Catheryn's apartment complex when he caught the sight of something out of the corner of his eye.

The vision startled him, causing him to fall back into the chair, his phone slipping from his grasp and bouncing across the floor. As he looked up, he noted the shadowy outline of a young woman standing there, in the dark, unmoving. He couldn't make out any of her features in the sparse light. Had someone broken in? He had other colleagues become the target of break-ins sometimes, in an attempt to steal drugs. The most frightening aspect was that they might be in a desperate, or irrational state when they did such a thing, so such confrontations had to be handled with caution. He had no weapons in the house, and the figure was between himself and easy reach of his phone. He took in a deep breath, doing his best to recall his continuing education training involving such issues.

"Hello?" he greeted, quietly. "Can I help you?"

The figure remained silent and unmoving. She seemed to be in profile, staring straight ahead toward the wall in front of her. She seemed to pay no attention to him, not responding to the sound of his voice.

"You are at 2245 Lexington Place. You have entered a private residence," he said, calmly, doing his best to recall the dialogue to use for such events.

"There are no narcotics or prescription drugs on the premises," he continued, softly.

The figure continued to stand in silence, unaffected by the doctor's words.

Faustus eased his hand over to the standing lamp just off the side of his arm chair, and very carefully, tilted the light in the direction of the intruder. More light spilled across the features of the young woman, still failing to respond to stimuli. She stood, frozen as David Faustus took in her clothing. Immediately, the business attire struck him as familiar. Catheryn had been wearing those same clothes that day. It gave him the bravado to pull the lamp even closer, and he gave out a sigh of relief. It was, indeed, Catheryn. But as to why she was standing there, unresponsive, unblinking, in the dark, was more than slightly bizarre.

"Catheryn!" he declared. "You scared the hell out of me. I've been trying to reach you all day—"

It was Faustus' turn to startle for a second time as Catheryn's face went slack-jawed, her eyes large with horror, her hand thrusting out before her toward the opposing wall.

And she screamed.

Faustus scurried up the back of his arm chair in complete shock, his gray eyes wide. The sound was terrifying, but it sounded so ethereal, so hollow—

almost as if feeding through an analog speaker. He didn't know what to make of it, other than something was very wrong here.

Before he could breathe another word, the figure seemed to melt back in to the shadows from where it had materialized, leaving the doctor in stunned silence. As reason started to return, he finally thought to lunge for his cell phone before slapping the switch for the overhead light of the bedroom. He spun about, ready to confront what might be there.

Empty. The room was empty. He was alone.

No. Not possible. Even though irrational, he flung open the door to the bathroom and checked inside. He checked the closet over by the arm chair, even though there was no possible way anyone could have moved that quickly. He stood by his bed, still trembling, trying to absorb what had just occurred.

When the phone in his hand rang, the adrenaline spike causing him to drop it. Cursing softly, he retrieved it, a shaking hand bringing the device to his ear. He took a moment to catch his breath.

"Dr. Faustus…hold—wait! Andrew? Slow down. I…just…meet me at the coffee shop across from the office. I'll be right there."

DARCIE McGRATH

6

The first thing Catheryn was aware of was the ringing in her ears. There was also a sense of bone-chilling dampness, but the ringing was the most blaring feature. As she found movement available to her limbs, she shifted in an attempt to sit upright. One hand went to her throbbing temple, and the other went to the ground to support her. There was the audible crunch of dead leaves beneath her, the crispness of the dried foliage working between her fingers.

She remembered something about screeching tires, a sudden lightness of being. She shifted her weight, trying to find the ability to stand, and as she did, she came to the realization she had no shoes on. So odd…

Her fingers trailed down the side of her face to her cheek as she had some memory of a sharp pain to the left side of her face. She drew her hand before her eyes, expecting to witness blood or some other kind of damage, but there was none. As she continued her self-examination, she found herself in a long white linen shift. She stretched out her arms, which appeared unscathed in the short-sleeved flax-spun garment. No wonder she was cold.

As she looked around her, she realized how dreary and dim the light of day appeared. She was surrounded by woods, and the woods themselves were enshrouded in some eerie mist. None of the branches carried the slightest hint of Spring. The ground was still littered with rotting dead oak and maple leaves. Without shoes, she was reluctant to step too quickly in fear what might lay underneath them, but she had enough of her scruples about her to realize she couldn't remain on the cold, wet ground.

Catheryn lurched toward a tree, the bark of the old oak rough against her hand. Had she tripped on something? She didn't recall anything under foot.

And that's when she heard the low, audible rumble. It travelled up through her ankles and sent her grappling for the support of the tree. Was there thunder, or was the ground, literally, shaking? She never thought of Iowa being earthquake territory, but they weren't too far from the fault at New Madrid.

She heard the snap of twigs near her, but it was the pale, haggard, emaciated face of an older woman peering down at her that sent her back to the ground and in to a full scurry under the protection of an ancient oak. The other woman's dark eyes were ringed with fatigue but also cold and vacant but with a tinge of fear about them. Her gray hair was in frazzled ringlets about her face; the rest of the strands were braided and secured beneath a white, pleated cap atop her head. She wore a gray, leather-laced stomacher-style bodice with an underlying white blouse of linen that was in desperate need of a laundering. The woman's long full gray petticoats spilled upon the forest floor as she leaned intrusively close in to Catheryn's personal space.

The older woman raised a single, bony finger to her own lips, uttering a long singular, "Shhhhh!"

The new arrival threw a frantic look over her shoulder to see if she had been followed. Satisfied that no one had, she returned her attention to Catheryn.

"Don't speak. Don't say a word," the woman whispered. "They'll hear us."

"Who will hear us?" Catheryn responded.

It was clear from the expression on the old woman's face that no tone of Catheryn's was ever going to be quiet enough. She shushed the injured woman again and scrambled to be tight next to her, peering through the mists of the woods in the most paranoid of fashions. Catheryn could still see nothing out of the ordinary.

"Who is out there?" the therapist pressed.

"The ghosts," the older woman squeaked. "You can't hear them?"

Confusion started to give way to panic as the doctor realized staying out here like this could result in hypothermic shock. Maybe that was why the old woman was so confused. She wasn't dressed much warmer than Catheryn. Maybe that's why her own head did not feel any clearer. Maybe hypothermia was setting in. Catheryn had to get help.

"...junction of Highway J-40 and 218. Requesting ambulatory connection to U of I..."

The voices sounded so far away. Catheryn was having a difficult time understanding them. And that nagging ringing in her ears...

"Hello?" she called out, rising from her position on the ground, her voice having a disturbing echo effect in the surrounding woods. "Can anyone hear me?"

"Quiet!" the old woman grated out, taking Catheryn's arm in a painful grip and dragging her back down into the leaves with her. "Do you want them to find us?!"

Catheryn shifted her attention back to the old woman, her hand raising up to the sallow cheek of the ashen face. It was ice cold.

"Are you alright? What's your name?"

"Mrs. Albert Alexander," the new arrival said, weakly. "My friends call me Lilly."

The younger woman smiled. "A pleasure to meet you, Lilly. My name is…is…"

She blinked as her thoughts evaporated into the air before her. Her name? Why couldn't she remember her name…She took a deep, steadying breath to bury the rising feeling of anxiety within her stomach. It was obvious that they were both in need of help.

The younger woman shifted her weight to pull the older woman up. "Maybe we need to get you some help—"

The frazzled woman stumbled back from the medium's touch as if it had burned her. "'Help'? What kind of 'help'? I've damaged the carriage. Do you realize what my husband will do when he finds me?"

"But if you're hurt—"

"No," the older woman muttered, nearly tripping on her own petticoats as she scrambled away from Catheryn. "No, no, no, no…nothing would be worse than the beating in store for me."

The woman fell to the forest floor, her hands covering her face, quietly weeping.

"I have nowhere to go. I fear he will kill me!"

The clarity of it hit the younger woman as she gazed down at the pitiful creature. She didn't know how she knew, but she just...did. The woman was dead, and she didn't know it. Perhaps as a result of the carriage accident she spoke of.

But Catheryn had *touched* her. The medium looked down at her own hands. She had felt the curve of the woman's cheek. The cold that radiated there from her aged, clammy skin...How did she do that? Where exactly was she?

Catheryn worked herself up from the ground, stepping toward the woman, and promptly tripped over a dead branch. She caught herself from falling by landing a hand on a nearby tree. The voices. What were the voices saying again? "Ambulatory". Was there an accident? She felt a pang of regret that someone else's misfortune might lead to her assistance.

"Hello!" the doctor yelled, louder.

It was no longer a low rumble this time. Catheryn rolled hard in to the tree. The aftershock was unmistakable. What was this! The world seemed to be quaking all around her. It didn't make sense.

The older woman fled from Catheryn's company, stumbling off in to the mists. The medium had to let her go. There was no helping her now. All she could do was help herself.

Catheryn listened carefully. The only answer she received was the same disturbing echo she had witnessed before. It was cold, so cold here. She began rubbing her arms in an effort to create any sort of warmth.

"…single car accident…victim is Caucasian, female…Illinois I.D. reads 'Greye, Catheryn', age 36…weak pulse…severe head trauma…"

She felt dizzy, and reached out for the support of the nearby tree, once more. Someone was transmitting a trauma report. How she knew that, she didn't know, but it was obvious someone was having a worse day than her. She felt guilty but she knew she had to get their attention. Unfortunately, she had no idea where the voices were coming from. They seemed to echo all around her; not too unlike her own voice. But, unlike her own voice, it seemed to fade and swirl all about her in an inconsistent manner. She couldn't get a bead on their direction.

"…waiving ambulatory connection…dispatch, we're going to need Airlift…"

That was when the light erupted from behind her. It was so bright that she had to hold her arm up to shield her eyes. She turned, resting her back against the tree to take in the full effect, continuing to keep her arm raised to protect her vision. Her green eyes grew incredulous at the bright, swirling mass before her. It had to be a staggering twenty feet tall, but as bright as it was, she could still see elements of the forest through it. She knew she should be wary of it, but it felt so…warm, almost comforting, somehow. She reached out questing fingers toward the anomaly, mesmerized by its beauty. Her heart ached. She wanted to go there. She needed to go there.

"…Dispatch, we're losing her!"

At those words, something seemed to permeate the field, reaching out and making contact with her hand. The jolt of it sent her reeling back in to the tree.

And, then, it all came flooding back.

She heard the screech of the tires first. The deer in the road. The feeling of going weightless. The pain. The pain in her head…

She snapped back, raising her arm to shield her eyes from the blinding light, finally recognizing it for what it was. Whatever had reached out to her was trying to inform her. Giving her the right to make a decision of something that could have been irreversibly permanent. To move forward had to be of her own free will.

But she wanted to go…the love, the unconditional love, enveloped her. Made her feel safe and warm like nothing in life ever had. Well, perhaps, once upon a time…

Almost upon that thought, the light receded, enclosing her in what appeared to be a darkened room. The light was not completely gone. There was enough to give the vague impression of dark walls and ceiling. She took a reluctant step forward into that small space. The movement appeared to trigger the echoing sound of plucked guitar strings; the stirrings of a sweet melody that brought memories flooding back to her of music. It reminded her of the evenings on the porch with her father, weaving a song through the night air and wrapping her in that blanket of warm affection she sorely missed from her childhood. Then, almost upon command, that presence was there. Seated in the darkness on that familiar wooden chair, and holding an acoustic guitar, was a familiar silhouette. The receding light was just enough that she could make out the familiar pastel plaid shirt, untucked, worn over faded blue jeans. The short hair was not the gray of his advanced years but the strawberry-blonde color of his middle years.

The sound of the guitar paused as if recognizing her approach, and there was a noticeable change in the silhouette as the head pivoted toward her.

"Caty-Girl…" There was a longing sign penetrating his words. "…my Caty Girl…not yet. It isn't time."

She dropped her arm, her face wet with tears. "Daddy?"

"Not yet," the voice repeated with soft affection.

And like a rubber band, the vision snapped away from her grasp, dissolving in to the murky setting of the woods. She was, once again, alone in the dark. She collapsed against the tree in wracking sobs, the warmth ripped away from her, and replaced with the brutal contrast of cold and dampness. But like a brisk splash of cold water, it brought her other senses to life.

Catheryn lifted her head, anxiety setting her body rigid against the tree. Something was there, watching. She could feel its invading, stalking presence. The being was in stark opposition to the loving presence found in the brightly-lit portal. It was its polar opposite. It had heard her, and it got her to wondering if the strange older woman wasn't so deranged after all. She felt a lump of fear forming in her throat. She was reluctant to turn toward it, as if any sudden moves might alert the predator to her position. She kept her body pressed against the sturdy oak, fear gripping her. It was colder than the cold, and it was encroaching on her position. She could hear a slight stirring of shuffling feet moving through the dead leaves. Squeezing her aventurine green eyes shut, she took a steady breath. She had to look. The need within her was overwhelming, as if her own safety depended on it.

She edged, ever so carefully around the tree, as to not give away her position. She strained her eyes to see around the rough-hewn bark of the mature oak, making the most of the tree as a barrier between herself and whatever was edging closer.

Catheryn could *feel* them before she saw them; cold, predatory logic exuding from its very being. They were numerous, but all seemed connected like a hive mind. Singular in thought and purpose—they were hungry.

Just out of the corner of her eyes, she could see them. They appeared wrapped in some ethereal fabric that ignored gravity, floating through the air as whisper silent as they did. Darker than dark, they used the shadows to blend and camouflage their stealthy movements. Not one branch cracked. Not one leaf crunched. She had no idea what they were, but she knew one thing for certain.

She could not let them find her.

She squeezed her eyes shut as fear encompassed her. No, don't be afraid. If her past taught her anything—if there was anything her father had taught her—such things were drawn to that emotion. How many late nights had her father been forced to do nightmare triage duty in her bedroom? She couldn't have been quite six years-old when the first of the dark things came. The things she learned quickly, out of necessity.

She made her breathing shallow, her back hard-pressed against the tree. She breathed in, and as she exhaled, she allowed the emotion to pass through into the tree. She imagined the tree absorbing the fear, traveling down the trunk and down into the root system. She visualized the energy dissipating harmlessly in to the earth, even as she felt the shadows passing by her position. She kept up the ritual, eyes closed, breathing quietly, allowing the energy of the emotion to pass through her and out. Feeling calmer, she slowly opened her eyes.

Only to find the dark shadow directly before her, its faceless blackness staring right in to her being.

Catheryn shrieked. Forgetting completely about the perils of the forest floor, she sprinted away, catching the silent army that had already passed her, completely unawares. A horrid shriek of their own went up; almost sounding like the collection of a choir of agony-laden screams all released at once.

She ran, sparing only brief glimpses behind her, and no thought to the debris beneath her feet. She remained focused on a singular goal—to get as much distance between the dark hoard and herself as she possibly could.

"...Dispatch, we have a pulse..."

She no longer paid heed to the echo of voices assaulting her from all directions. She had no time for them as she ran toward what she knew not what. All she knew was that she had lost all hope that they could help her. She was on her own.

It was at that moment that another sound came in to her awareness. Hoofbeats. The gaining hoofbeats of a horse. She cringed, pressing onward, not daring to look, praying that her pursuers had not found faster transport.

An arm snatched her around the waist. Before she could utter a shriek, she found herself stomach-down on the saddle of a horse. The strength in which she was lifted seemed unmistakably male, but nothing was beyond possibility in this strange place. She strained to look up, but all she could see was the fluttering beige canvas flaps of a duster trailing behind them. She took some relief in the fact that her capturer was not wearing black, and that the dark figures appeared to all but vanish behind them.

But was this individual her rescuer, or something worse?

DARCIE McGRATH

7

Beanie's, 4th and Central, Chicago, Illinois, USA

"I was in bed. Sound asleep. Early morning showing, you know? And then I looked up, and she was standing right there!"

It was obvious to Faustus that Andrew was clearly shaken to leave his apartment looking in such a state. The realtor was still in his pair of plaid pajama bottoms, heather gray t-shirt, and not one ounce of product in his blonde hair. Even without it, it seemed to be sticking out at odd angles all over his head—a stark difference from the perfectly-polished portfolio headshots on his promotional sales material.

The senior therapist allowed the agent to continue his rant, noting through the shaking of the young man's hands on the forest green Formica tabletop that the two cups of coffee he had ordered for them was probably the last thing Baldwin needed at the moment.

"She was just...*standing* there, not saying anything, and then all the sudden she just—screamed! Scared the bejesus out of me!" he declared.

The younger man's highly-animated hands finally landing on top of his bedhead of blond hair.

"And then she just…vanished! Did I just see her ghost?!" he whispered anxiously, leaning conspiringly toward the therapist across the table. "Is she…dead?"

Faustus blinked, trying to ground himself from being dragged in to Baldwin's paranoia.

"If she is, whispering won't help. She could still hear you."

The doctor cringed, realizing too late that now was not the time for a teaching moment as the sales agent threw his hands down on the table, shoving his body back in to the green faux leather booth in a clear sign of agitation.

Faustus relaxed back in to the green faux leather booth, his fingers wrapped around his cup of coffee, brow furrowed in thought.

"No, I don't think so," he muttered, taking a sip, not sure if what he said was the truth, or more of a fervent wish.

But, something, deep down, resonated truth.

"I think what we witnessed was a crisis apparition."

Andrew blinked. "A crisis…what?"

The therapist focused his gray eyes at his shaken companion. "A crisis apparition is a psychic projection spontaneously sent to loved ones at time of crisis."

Andrew's expression changed to curiosity. "You mean like my Uncle Bob showing up in my bedroom to say goodbye, before my aunt told me the next morning that he had passed away?"

Faustus had to fight down a half-smile. Very rarely could he have these kinds of conversations with just anyone. Someone...experienced. For Andrew Baldwin, this was not unusual. For him, this was just Sunday.

"No, that's a deathbed visitation. That happens after our loved ones pass on and they visit before they go..." Faustus paused, taking another sip from his cup. "Well...wherever they go on to. Crisis apparitions are usually projected from the Living."

"So, wherever she is, she's still alive?"

"As of an hour ago, yes."

Andrew abruptly stood up from the booth. "Well, we gotta find her. Where is she?"

The therapist stayed seated. "I don't know."

Andrew blinked at him, incredulously. "What do you mean you don't know..."

"I've been trying to call her all day," Faustus replied, defensively. "All calls have gone to voice mail."

Faustus scratched at the scruff on his chin as if to raise the spirit of inspiration. It seemed to work. The doctor snapped his finger as the recollection struck him.

"Catheryn gave me a key to her apartment in case something like this should come up. I've never used it. Now, seems like a good time."

"Well, what are we waiting for," the enthusiastic real estate agent declared. "Let's go!"

"Thank you, Officer, for your time. I'll be looking forward to hearing back from you."

David Faustus dropped the cell phone in to his tweed coat pocket, as Andrew Baldwin emerged from Catheryn's bedroom. He hoped the realtor had better news than he received from local law enforcement.

"Anything?" the doctor asked.

Andrew shrugged, shaking his head, confused. "She appears to have packed in a hurry. Her stuff is kinda thrown all over. That purple roller bag she travels with appears to be missing."

Faustus stroked his two-day old stubble, thoughtfully, hoping for inspiration to strike twice. No go.

"Where could she have gone?" the older man muttered.

A wince seemed to creep up on Baldwin's face. "I think…I might know."

Faustus frowned. The cringe in the smaller man's demeanor looked familiar—the look of a man that might be in for a sound beating.

"Out with it."

"I told her Bramden House had been put up for sale."

"*What?!*" David Faustus stared down at the real estate agent, stunned. "And you didn't think to bring this up sooner?"

"It didn't seem to matter at the time," Andrew said, defensively, his tightened shoulders slumping in defeat. "…until now."

The senior therapist paced before the picture window of Catheryn's living room, raising a hand to his temple to massage it between his thumb and fingers.

"I may have to call Officer Branley back," he muttered with a frown. "I don't know if this will help—or hinder—this case."

A flicker of an idea seemed to cross Faustus' gaunt features.

"We need to get back to the office," he said, hurriedly, heading for the front door of the apartment.

The cab had Faustus and Baldwin at the office in a mere matter of minutes. It would have taken quite a bit longer had it been a weekday.

Faustus keyed in to the office alarm and slapped the lights as Baldwin came in to the doorway, panting. Faustus may have had a decade on the realtor, but the senior partner was definitely more fit.

Faustus already had Catheryn's laptop open, when the realtor came up from behind to watch at his shoulder.

"You know her password?" Andrew asked, curiously.

"Of course," Faustus muttered, typing in the access and bringing up the desktop. "The equipment belongs to the practice. Sometimes patient notes don't always get transferred to the share drive. She has access to mine, too. Although…"

The doctor, clicked a few more shortcuts, bringing up Catheryn's browser window.

"…I do know she has a tendency to misplace her phone," his spoken thought process slowed down by the typing. "And, she's used the browser search before…Yes! The account is still logged in. Here it is."

Andrew watched as the computer screen brought up a map of the local area, and as the software pinged away, the search map grew.

The realtor frowned. "This doesn't always work…sometimes it doesn't cross networks…"

Faustus did his best to wait patiently as the system continued to ping for the phone. It wasn't looking promising, but at least it wasn't finding it in the local vicinity.

Which only left, the rest of the world.

The senior doctor sighed, his mind racing. He pursed his lips in agitation.

"There's always the ring feature. It will ring for 5 minutes until someone picks up," Andrew offered, anxiously. "If the battery is still active."

The senior doctor activated the system option on the computer. The phone rang, the map zeroing in on the wayward signal. It rang again. On the third ring, it stopped.

Someone must have activated the phone to make the ringing stop. The map began to zoom in, its map marker dropping in an ominous location that made Faustus frown.

Baldwin leaned over his shoulder. "University of Iowa hospital campus?"

Faustus' mind rolled through his memories. He had been there, once, for a conference. It was a large campus. But at least it gave them a place to start, and his credentials might work to their advantage.

Calling the information phone number only bounced him off a few switch boards before he found a human willing to speak with him. All Andrew Baldwin could do was anxiously wait at his shoulder.

"This is Dr. David Faustus. I understand you have Dr. Catheryn Greye there. I'm a colleague of Dr. Greye's. May I speak to her, please?"

The look of concern in Dr. Faustus' eyes when he chanced to look up at Andrew did not inspire confidence in the younger man.

"I see," the doctor muttered, his expression turning grave. "When was this? Last evening…Is it possible to speak to her attending?"

Andrew did not like to be left out of the conversation, searching David Faustus' face, anxious for answers.

The senior therapist shut down the phone, unable to meet the realtor's gaze.

"There's been an accident. She's in intensive care at University of Iowa," Faustus muttered. "She's in a coma."

8

The first thing that registered with Catheryn was the sunlight on her eyelids. She opened them, immediately averting her gaze from the glare. She was in a bed, with quilts tucked about her. She shifted, using one hand to struggle to sit upright and using the other to fend off the bright light streaming through the window directly across from her. Someone in the room moved to pull a curtain over to dim the discomfort, and Catheryn felt someone sit down in a chair to her right. Her mouth felt full of cotton, and she was grateful to hear someone pouring a glass of water in anticipation of her need.

A young, unfamiliar woman smiled down at Catheryn from her bedside. The purple, tiny flower-print cotton day dress she was wearing was protected by a white, pinner-style apron. Her long brown hair was meticulously pinned up and covered by a white lace day cap. She may have looked like a woman out of time, but her warm smile was still very welcome. As she moved to receive the glass from her gracious host, another figure loomed in to view, standing over the attendant, and the sight of him nearly caused Catheryn to drop the glass of water on to the bed.

Catheryn let out an anxious gasp as she struggled to scramble back away from the visitor. His green-gray eyes, weathered face, and straw-like blonde hair had haunted her nightmares for months, but instead of the leering look of evil and distain, his energy and expression truthfully radiated a feeling of genuine concern.

A fleeting shadow of regret mixed with acceptance passed over the face of Jackson Carter as the caregiver next to her leapt in to action in an attempt to steady her.

"Please know, Ms. Catheryn that I mean no harm," the quiet familiar tenor voice drawled. "I just happened to be in the neighborhood when I noticed your distress. I'm sorry if I spooked ya."

Catheryn still found it difficult to accept the charitable disposition of Carter a thing of reality, and found it difficult to remove her pale green eyes from him, even as she accepted the young woman's assistance in propping her upright.

Her memories came creeping back, slowly. The white porcelain pitcher and washbowl at the bed stand. The tall ornate oak headboard of the bed.

The matching set of dresser drawers to the right of her.

And if there was any doubt of where she was, framed by the antique glass across from her, was the view of the pedestrian bridge crossing the Des Moines River, the morning sun dancing upon the current as it flowed on to the Mississippi. No other place could fill her with such tranquility, and there was no other place she would be happier to regain her strength than Bramden House.

Of course, the beauty of the memory was marred by the standing presence to her right.

"Please don't mind Mr. Carter, Ms. Catheryn," her attendant said softly, her doe-like eyes pleading with her for understanding. "I know his past has been most troublesome, but he has been quite …indispensable to us. He's done much to make reparations for his misdeeds."

Jackson Carter's gaze stayed floor-bound, fussing with the brown slouch hat in his hands.

"I appreciate your kind words, Ms. Anna, but my debt to Ms. Catheryn…" The hired hand's hazel eyes met the therapist's gaze ever so briefly. "…is, understandably, a work in progress."

An older, matronly woman of small, stout stature entered the room from the hallway to Catheryn's left. She wore her dark hair, streaked with gray, up in a tight bun. Her white cotton blouse sported a high neck with lace trim and a bib-style front popular in the late 1800's. Her gray skirt was a straighter style, and not as full-looking as the younger girl attending to her.

"Apologies for the interruption," the older woman announced with an air of pleasant authority that reminded Catheryn of her own grandmother. "Mr. Carter, would you mind collecting the doctor from downstairs?"

Carter only offered a slight nod to Catheryn with a quiet, "Ma'am," before exiting the room.

With the distraction gone, the therapist's attention came back to more present questions. She turned her mystified expression on the young woman next to her.

"I don't understand," Catheryn breathed. "How can I be here? I thought all of you to be gone from this place…"

The woman only smiled warmly, her dimpled cheeks drawing light up to dance in her dark eyes. Even so, there was a hint of withholding behind that brightness.

The conversation was interrupted by the heavy footsteps of boots on barnwood traveling down the hallway toward the room. Catheryn's heart leapt. There was no mistaking the energy behind those footfalls. She knew exactly who it was without seeing them. As she listened, a curiously-fast series of steps seemed to overtake the other footsteps and a small, elderly man in a black frock coat and matching Stetson, burst in to the room. The new arrival placed an antique brown doctor's bag next to Catheryn's bed, and perched his hat on a spindle of the wash stand behind him, revealing a thinning head of silver hair. He produced an old-style stethoscope with a bell-shaped head from inside his frock and strung the article about his neck. This was obviously, the long-awaited doctor. At least she hoped so as he took her wrist and felt about for her pulse. Apparently satisfied with the results, a pair of wizened blue eyes peered over the top of wire-rimmed spectacles to meet hers.

"Hello, Ms. Catheryn. I'm Dr. Coyle."

Another set of footfalls entered the room, causing the physician to arch a perturbed bushy eyebrow. He addressed the individual without turning around.

"I'd greet you with the time of day," the old man continued, placing the black ends of the stethoscope in to each ear. "...but, some of us like to argue about what time of the day that *is*."

The familiar brooding presence came up short in the entry way, black cavalry boots pausing at the oak-timbered doorframe. Catheryn's eyes followed up the cavalry boots, past the sky-blue trousers and dark blue shell jacket. Uncomfortably intense dark eyes regarded the doctor from that position. He muttered a curse from under his signature thick dark moustache, swiping his leather-trimmed kepi hat from his head of thick dark hair, and tucking it under one arm.

"Who let *him* in here?!" Captain Charles Danforth demanded of the young female attendant seated next to the bed.

The young, doe-eyed assistant stiffened in her chair, almost to the point of attention. "I…I…"

"Oh, leave the poor girl alone, you brute," the doctor drawled casually, placing the bell-shaped stethoscope head to Catheryn's chest. "She's only doing her job. Anna, dear, why don't you go down to the kitchen and prepare a poultice."

The young girl didn't need any further excuse. The spectral officer made room in the doorframe as the purple-flowered dress swept by.

"She doesn't need a poultice, you quack," Danforth retorted. "Is that stupid poultice your answer to everything?"

"That poultice would have saved your life had I been here when you were alive." The elderly doctor spared a glance over his shoulder. "Still missing the war, are we? You'd think you'd find something else to wear. Or, do you just enjoy bossing people around with that get-up."

The officer's face darkened. "That poultice isn't going to fix anything she's got!"

"I was giving the poor girl an excuse to leave. I'm going to join her!" Dr. Coyle stood abruptly, removing the antique instrument from around his neck and stuffing it inside his frock coat before turning to Catheryn. "I'll be around if you need me, Ms. Catheryn. Feel free to send for me."

"Don't worry," Danforth snorted. "She *won't*."

The doctor moved to the doorframe, pausing to lock eyes with the spectral officer. If either flinched, Catheryn didn't see it. Not a word was exchanged as the doctor went upon his way.

His ire fading, it was now Danforth's turn to feel uncomfortable. Eyes lowered, he raked his fingers through his mess of thick dark hair, recently exposed by the removal of his hat. He cleared his throat in an effort to remove the gruffness from his voice, finally finding it within himself to meet her gaze.

"You alright?" he muttered.

"Did you arrange this?" she replied.

"'Arrange' what?"

"*This!*" she said, somewhat exasperated, throwing her hands up to gesture around her. "Did you bring me here?"

"No…" Charlie Danforth blinked at her, suddenly finding himself scrambling for words. "Jackson was returning from the other house on your side of the Veil, and he found you in the woods. *He* brought you here."

The captain closed his eyes, attempting to clear his thoughts with an expelled breath. "I wish he hadn't."

Catheryn blinked. "You wish he hadn't *found* me?"

He shook his head, gruffly. "No! I…"

He raked a frustrated handful of fingers through his hair once more, for lack of anything else to say. He was floundering in his thoughts. He let his hand fall to wipe the uncertainty of his expression from his face, his fingers poised over his mouth until he found words to say. He winced, wrapping his fingers around the back of his neck.

"You shouldn't be here."

The medium blinked. A thousand times she had thought about what to say to him. What he might say to her. This was far from the mark where she had thought those words would land.

Her gaze landed in the comforter. "I missed you, too."

9

Surgical Care Unit, University Hospitals, Iowa City, Iowa, USA

Andrew Baldwin never could appreciate hospitals in general, let alone at night. He was grateful he opted for the long sleeve gray Henley he wore. It was made of the waffle-knit cotton thermal fabric that constructed most long underwear. The room was cold and he found himself in a near-fetal position in the green vinyl-covered chair at the foot of the hospital bed. Faustus slept in an identical chair at his partner's bedside. The nurse was kind enough to supply pillows, which propped up the senior therapist's head at odd angles in the inflexible, block-style chair. Baldwin couldn't imagine how stiff the doctor's neck would be in the morning.

The real estate agent gazed at the patient in the bed. It was difficult to look upon Catheryn with the heavy bruising and scars on her body and face, but it was also something about all the tubes, cables, and wires invading her arms, head and body. Even with all of the terrors he had witnessed with the duo in the last year, this vision ranked up there as one of the most disturbing.

The time in the room gave Baldwin a moment to reflect how Catheryn and his relationship had changed in one year's time. His sales-to-list ratio was above 95-percent, with an average days-on-market beneath 50. He was multilingual; tops in regional sales 4 years in a row. "Medium" just never seemed to fit on the business card; yet, admittedly, he saw to it with less care than the rest of his life skills. But seeing how Catheryn had integrated that aspect of herself with reverence and sense of duty impressed him. So much of his life had been rather ruthless; in direct competition with others in his field. When Catheryn offered to take him under her wing—to help him—it caught him off-guard. But he knew, just by the integrity in which she worked at the house in the Des Moines River Valley, that her offer was genuine.

He owed Catheryn a large debt. She had helped bring stability to those aspects of his personal life that he had neglected. It helped ground him emotionally and spiritually in a way he couldn't begin to thank her for.

And, he was no more grateful to her than he was at that moment. Hospitals were often alive with multitudes of the Dead looking for attention. Thanks to Catheryn, she had taught him enough grounding and shielding techniques to keep the hospital room quiet.

But he was still far from physically comfortable with his surroundings to just fall asleep. The lights had been turned down for night, but a large bright LED screen on the wall blared Catheryn's personal information, vitals, and attending hospital staff data. The support devices attached to her clicked and whirred, with the occasional odd alarm that would make Andrew jump. In stark contrast, Faustus snoozed away, oblivious to it all.

"Well, ma," he muttered in an odd attempt to amuse himself. "They haven't pulled out the leeches yet, so we must be in one of those *good* hospitals."

Andrew glanced out toward the hallway. Any hustle and bustle outside the room was kept to a minimum by the thick door, but he could still make out the movement of the evening's activity by the shadows darting around underneath it. The ballasts in the hallway ceiling were turned down to half-light to allow for the patients' sleeping comfort in the evening, but the one just outside the door was annoyingly dysfunctional. The light flickered, on and off, as if it couldn't quite decide what its state was to be. It was out of place in the high-tech, pristine condition of the facility. An oversight by maintenance, perhaps? Maybe if he went to the nurses' station to talk about it...

He slipped out in to the hall, allowing the soft-close mechanism to shut the industrial-sized door behind him. The light continued to flicker intermittently above his head, casting eerie shadows along the corridor that would probably be completely non-threatening in normal light of day. At night, it just gave the unsettling effect of a cheap horror movie. He did his best to dismiss it as he padded his way down the carpeted hallway toward the station.

It was quiet. Just too quiet for his comfort. The halls had been busy all day with gurneys, equipment, orderlies and nurses dashing to and fro. He expected it to be a little less during the night shift, but not this…absent. It just added to his unease.

And then, there was the *cold*. He couldn't pinpoint where it was coming from. Was it a draft or just the ambient temperature? He wondered if that would be good for Catheryn's health. Maybe he should ask the nurse for another blanket…or five.

There it was. He knew he wasn't imagining it now. It was moving. He felt it. The cold from…wherever it came from…whirled about his body. It startled him to the point that he jumped to look behind him. Nothing. Just the irritating light flickering oddly away in the corridor. Something wasn't right here. He stretched out his extra sense around him. He turned to continue his way down the hall.

When it materialized right in front of him.

He jumped backward. He not only felt the cold; he saw the origin of it. It was dark. It was an unmistakable shadow darting across the hallway, right in front of him. It was almost testing him—daring him—to notice it. There was no question. He saw it.

His hazel eyes wide, he backed away. He stifled a shriek when it did it again, right before him. It was taunting him. Terrifying him. Almost as if it knew it could. It swept across his vision, again, but this time, the movement was accompanied by a sensation across his bare neck. This was hot; a burning along the collar of his gray Henley. His mind, frantically, flipped through the rolodex of Catheryn's training. He didn't know what this was, but that part wasn't important. What was important was how he reacted to it.

The darkness exploded in to a plume of black smoke before him, growing larger and larger until it was the shape of a massive cloud. It loomed above him in a frightening manner, skimming the ceiling tiles above them.

It was at that moment a night-shift nurse poked her head over the counter of the nurses' station, most likely in response to the realtor's repressed howl. Seeing Andrew, she rose sharply and quickly ventured out from behind the counter. The light of the station backlit the nurse, showing off the silhouette of a female in scrubs.

"Sir, can I help you?" she called.

Her voice lacked any urgency, but seemed to express an air of annoyed curiosity of why a man would be standing in the middle of an urgent care facility making noise at three in the morning. It was clear that she did not see what he was seeing.

However, that was *not* the same reaction provided by the other nurse rounding the corner from the connecting corridor. The African-American nurse with short, curly hair and pink scrubs turned toward Andrew and froze in mid-stride. Even in the dim light of the hallway, he could read the terror etched across her features, her mouth opening and closing as she observed the mass growing between them. Her chest heaved in hyperventilating gasps, drawing the attention of the station nurse away from Andrew.

The nurse moved toward her compatriot. "Bonnie? Bonnie! Are you okay?"

The other nurse's brown eyes were wide, fixated on the billowing, churning mass before her.

"Don't you see it?" she shrieked, frozen in place, arms splayed wide as if fighting her fight-or-flight instincts.

"See what!" the other nurse demanded, urgency creeping in to her voice; less to do with what she could see but more from the reaction of her colleague.

The nurse named Bonnie finally found her courage to move and bolted down the hall to pick up an exhausted Baldwin from the carpeted floor. As if sensing an attack, the plume of blackness shot straight up through the ceiling, causing both the stunned nurse and stricken man to stare upward. As it became apparent the thing was no longer going to regroup and attack again, the nurse eased a shocked Baldwin on to his feet. As she did so, she noticed his neck. Right above the collar of the Henley were four prominent wounds—scratches.

"Oh my God," she breathed.

"Did you see it?" Andrew asked, his breath ragged. "Did you *see it*?!"

The nurse didn't say a word, but after a moment's hesitation, frantically nodded.

"Bonnie!" the other nurse called. "What's going on!"

The nurse at Baldwin's side allowed him to rest his weight against her until the man could find his feet on his own. She used that moment of intimacy to whisper to him.

"Don't worry," Nurse Bonnie said in hushed tones. "I *think* I know what to do."

The frantic nurse turned her attention back over her shoulder. "It's okay. I thought he was having an episode. He's alright!"

The nurse continued to help Andrew along the corridor, one arm around him to support him. "Let's get you back to your room."

10

Danforth rested the palms of his hands on the white frame of the glass window facing the river. Catheryn's room was the most comfortable of the house; the view overlooking the river, bridge and main street of the town. She was out of bed today. Misty, one of the servant girls, had loaned her one of her prettier-style wrapper garments that allowed Catheryn something fresh to wear, and they were able to make it outside to take in the sunshine. It was from that vantage that Danforth watched them, concern etched under his dark eyes.

The house assistant, Anna, found him like that. She sighed resignedly, wiping her sun-kissed hands on the pinner apron attached to her white and blue plaid cotton day dress. She moved to his side. He made no acknowledgement, so she stood silently, next to him for a time, taking in the view with him. It was clear that she would have to be the one to break the silence.

"Have you spoken to her, yet?" she said to the window pane.

The officer released a tired sigh, resting his entire weight on to the palms of his hands.

"No. What am I supposed to say?"

Anna blinked slowly, calmly, at him with her brown eyes. "Something is better than nothing at all."

"You don't know what I know." He shook his head, his tired gaze falling to the window sill. "I wish I didn't."

"Perhaps I don't, but her heart is breaking. Surely, you must feel that." She searched his face, concerned, trying to draw upon his attention. "Would you have rather Jackson just…left her out there?"

"Of course, not," he whispered. "If he hadn't collected her, I would have."

She could feel his longing, his wanting to be there next to her, but as transparent as his feelings were, she didn't understand them. They conflicted so completely with his actions.

"Out of all of the living visitors ever to come to this house—none of them have impacted me as greatly as she," he muttered, his eyes fixed upon her once more.

"Because she can see you—"

"No…she's not the first I've ever met that could do that." He chuckled, haughtily, at the window sill. "Most those mediums…they were just pushy voyeurs and busybodies. Couldn't quote *me* to save their lives."

He found a new grip on both sides of the window, finding a new view to continue watching them move down the street.

"She was the first," he mumbled. "I felt her before she even got here."

"You've felt others before they've come here before."

"Yes, but *she* found *me*."

His hand slid from the window frame and settled, absentmindedly, over where his heart had been. Regardless of its absence, he still felt it there—that first moment her energy had first touched his. He closed his eyes. It exhilarated him and made him ache at the same time. He recalled the meeting with her guide in the attic—how the elevated being had showed him the multiple paths to nowhere that such a relationship would lead. Some of the potential outcomes were outright terrifying.

Then, why, in the name of all that was holy, had she been allowed to come here? Was he in Hell and he just happened to miss the turn at the road sign? He promised her guide not to interfere with her life; not to pursue any further intimacy with her.

Yet, *she*, continually, reached out to *him*.

Her essence reached out to him, even in the dream state, in her loneliness, yearning to be with him. It was enticing and captivating, and there were times he came close to succumbing to the beautiful glow that was her. She had such a giving, nurturing, selfless spirit. He didn't understand how a whole world could miss that, or if they did notice her, it was those that would take advantage. All he could do was share in her victories and do his best to cheer her, from afar, but he was more keenly aware of her pain. He felt every ache in her being every time someone would reject her. Could feel her agony as she cried herself to sleep at night as her loneliness consumed her. It drew him to her, naturally; his presence there in less than a heartbeat. If only he could comfort her, just enough for her to know that he was there. But no. The memory of the nightmarish visions shown to him would dance before his eyes, and he would stop short.

Well, most of the time.

But the only thing giving her comfort was a single dance on a patio under the moonlight on a fall day. And how he ached to do it, again.

Why? Why was he to be the one to bear the burden of this knowing, alone? What their future would hold…Why have her suffer? Why would they not tell *her* the hopelessness of it all?

His thoughts were disrupted by the commotion down in the entryway.

The two of them had returned from their walk.

He pulled away from the window. "I need to go."

"But, Captain—"

Anna's pained expression said all that was needed.

"Please see to it that she is attended to," he muttered, turning toward the door. "I will be on my rounds."

Anna felt the cloud of torment leave with him, leaving her to only sigh again, albeit, this time, in frustration. But, as he passed, she noticed something peculiar. She moved out in to the hallway, observing him descending the staircase. He never bothered with the stairs. His ethereal form was no longer in need of them.

Catheryn, still very much engrained in the needs and patterns of her physical life, gravitated to take the stairs to the second floor. There was a moment of surprise as she looked up to see him there; a brief exchange of glances as he passed by her.

And, a slight touch as he moved by. All of what could have been, strategically, avoided had he simply passed his ethereal form through the barnwood floor.

But, he didn't.

Anna smiled. It gave her a feeling of hope that perhaps the tension in the house may finally be lifted from all who dwelled within.

11

The knock on the hospital room door startled Andrew Baldwin out of a sound sleep. Faustus was already awake, freshly-shaven and in a new change of clothes. The doctor made it to the door first and was more than taken aback by the appearance of the character at the door.

There stood a bespectacled male, about five foot nine, dressed in a very dated tan tweed coat and trousers. The disarray of his short light brown hair was contained by a brown bowler hat, and both his chin and his full moustache were in need of a trim. But there was no mistaking the smile that reached all the way up to his hazel eyes that greeted them.

"Did someone call for the chaplain?" he called, cheerfully.

Andrew rose as the individual entered the room but immediately regretted the sudden movement as it strained the injury at his neck. The agent winced, his hand rising to the pain point. He forgot that the nurse had bandaged his wounds before he retired for the night.

The new arrival seemed to take note of the injury right away.

"Hmm, you must be Andrew," the spectacled man mused, moving without permission to touch the bandage at Baldwin's neck. "This doesn't bode well."

The visitor seemed to noticed the curious looks of the conscious residents of the room.

"Oh, I'm sorry!" he muttered, fingering the lapels of his tweed jacket. "I was at a historical event down the street when I got the message. I do historical reenacting sometimes. I thought I'd best get here right away. Bonnie rarely calls for *general* ministry needs."

David crossed the room to shake the chaplain's hand. "Dr. Faustus. A pleasure, Father...err..."

"'Pastor Daniel' will do."

"'Pastor', thank you," Faustus smiled. "I'm afraid I wasn't awake when the events happened, so I will leave Mr. Baldwin to explain."

The pastor listened, stroking his unshaven chin, thoughtfully, as Andrew recounted the events of the early morning.

"I see," the little man mused. "I'm familiar. I have certain...sensitivities...you see. It runs in my family; all the way back to my great-great grandfather. It's his persona I portray most of the time. He was a vicar—a chaplain with the 116th Illinois during the American Civil War."

"So, you have experience with things like this??" Andrew asked, frustratedly. "You know what this is?"

"Some people call it a wraith, but my great-grandfather talked about such things in his journals," the chaplain explained. "He called it the Coldness. It seemed to wander the battle fields and the surgical tents. It never took a definitive form…but you could always feel the cold."

David Faustus' gray eyes narrowed perceptively. "You think these things are real?"

"Oh, they've been reported by hospital staff, police officers, nurses, patients…for…centuries now," the visitor explained. "They're thought to feed off the weakened state of people that are not strong enough to fight back."

"Are they…human?" Faustus asked.

The pastor frowned. "Not sure. They do seem to respond to religious provocation, though."

Andrew felt a chill roll through him as he cast a glance over at the unmoving form of Catheryn lying in the bed.

"Can they…kill?" Andrew asked, not certain he wanted the answer.

The pastor's grim expression told him all he needed to know.

The agent locked his hazel eyes with Faustus. "We've gotta protect her!"

The two men's attention turned to the chaplain.

"What do we do?" Andrew asked, firmly.

The little man's face was solemn but determined.

"They are easily attracted to those that glow; those with abilities," he answered, candidly. "Likely why it struck out at you, Andrew."

Andrew chuckled, perplexed. "Why me?"

"You can see it, which makes you both a benefit and a threat. You're easier to terrify so it can scare you away. It can take whatever form it needs to scare you," the pastor said, matter-of-factly. "But it also means you can identify it and react. It could dance a jig in front of the doctor here, and it wouldn't do a thing." He directed his last thought toward the senior therapist. "No offense, Dr. Faustus."

Faustus arched a perturbed eyebrow before terminating the action with a resigned sigh. The holy man may have lacked tact but he had to admit that the pastor wasn't wrong.

"None taken," Faustus relented.

"So…" Andrew shrugged. "What do we do?"

"Well, we're going to need bait."

Faustus bristled. "Catheryn is out of the question!"

The little man smiled. "Oh, I would never *dream* of using Dr. Greye."

That was when both men turned to Andrew Baldwin.

Andrew looked pained. "Oh, you've got to be kidding!"

"Hey there! Mister…Wraith!!" Baldwin called out down the dim, empty hall way, throwing his hands up in complete lack of confidence that he was even doing it right.

He was certain his presentation, from the outside observer, looked completely comical. How did one address such a thing? Did they have names? Could he even pronounce it if it did? He was sensing limited potential for a reality television show in his future.

"Here I am!" the blonde-haired agent alerted, with an awkward shrug.

Pastor Daniel had worked out a deal with Nurse Bonnie to have control of the hallway for about an hour. Beyond that, she doubted she could keep the rotating staff out of the area. Whatever they did, they'd have to do it quick.

Andrew couldn't believe he was doing this. To think that the only thing that terrified him two years ago was making a drunken spectacle of himself at the junket in Cabo San Lucas. Now, here he was; offering himself as bait to a dark lethal entity to save his friend.

Of course, he didn't know which was more incredulous in that statement—the fact that he was saving his friend from a dark entity, or the fact that he had an *actual* friend. Sadly, his life had been all about career to this point. 'Friendships' were something to be used. Bartered.

Now, he actually had a friendship he wouldn't trade for anything, and he'd best renew his focus if he was to *keep* that friend.

He threw up his arms in exasperation. He couldn't yell all night, or in this case—morning. The patients might send up complaints and could cost Bonnie and Pastor Daniel their jobs.

"Come on, man," Andrew muttered under his breath. "I'm right here!"

A critical life systems alarm split the silence of the ward. It was from right behind him. As he honed in on the location, his blood ran cold.

It was Catheryn's room.

He noticed a flash of pink scrubs as Nurse Bonnie rushed past him. He followed her and came up short to avoid colliding with her. She was frozen as if the iciness that permeated the room had nailed her in place; her mouth agape as they both witnessed the familiar black cloud roiling above Catheryn's bed. Pastor Daniel had his book out with his cross held before him, while Faustus was pressed back in to his chair by the abrupt arrival of all in the room. The doctor's eyes swept the room, desperately straining to see anything that the others were seeing.

The pastor stood his ground, his booming voice heard above the claxon of the alarm as he thrust the cross before him.

"I call upon St. Michael the Archangel to cast out this menace!"

The blackness pulled back just far enough for the nurse to find her nerve. She was on the critical support fluids, rechecking all the vitals.

"I don't know what's wrong!" the nurse cried out.

The books that were set on the table across the room flew off, nearly striking the senior therapist in the head.

"...calling upon the Armies of God to rid us of this pestilence!"

"Andrew, do something!" Faustus barked, finally launching himself from the chair, ready to do battle with the unseen foe. "It's killing her!"

The chill in the room manifested into a whipping wind that wrapped and pulled the drapes of the window to a near ripping point. The flowers sent by well-wishers launched like missiles in the direction of the pastor who ducked them, completely unphased and continuing unabated.

Baldwin's fists were frustrated balls of fury. "God damn, you! Take on *me*, you coward!"

Faustus was frustrated. He couldn't see it, but he had three sets of eyes in the room to pick a vector. In the middle of the din, he found himself purchased on top of the chair seat and screamed directly in to the space above Catheryn with all of the strength he could muster.

"GET THE HELL OUTTA HERE YOU ASSHOLE!!"

To the team's surprise, the black mass recoiled sharply away from the doctor's explosive delivery, twisting about violently, and plunging through the far wall. The hurricane winds that had whipped the room, ceased abruptly, the drapes settling, calmly, back in to place.

Eyes turned to a winded Dr. Faustus who was still catching his breath, hands on the knees of his slacks, still standing atop the seat cushion. The only noise in the room was the blare of the critical system alarm. The young nurse reached over to address it, but as she did, the system dropped to normal readings. She scrambled over the patient and checked vitals manually, looking mystified.

"There's nothing wrong here," she muttered. "I don't get it."

Andrew could only blink, incredulously, at Faustus. "Damn, Doc!"

The senior therapist let out a labored sigh as the pastor helped him down from his perch. Once down, the pastor turned to take the younger man's shoulders in a gentle, but firm, grip.

"Andrew—don't you *ever* say that again. You never invite the power of Darkness upon yourself!" the holy man said, firmly.

"Sure," Andrew said, rolling his eyes. "I'll remember that next infestation."

"Is it gone?" Faustus asked, his eyes nervously darting about.

"No," the pastor stated, glumly. "We just drove it off for now."

12

Catheryn looked up from her book when the white rose drifted down on to the table top. It was a curious arrival to simply…drop from the air.

She had suffered a night of horrible dreams. She was reliving the chase through the woods, but this time, it was different. While before she was able to elude the dark, frightening wraiths, there seemed no one to stave off their pursuit of her this time. Pressing her back against the rough bark of the tree, she didn't dare breathe, but as she turned to see if she had shaken her pursuers, the tattered hood of the relentless hunter thrust itself before her vision. She opened her mouth to scream, but a bony hand thrust forward, seizing her neck. She couldn't utter a sound. She couldn't breathe.

And that was how she woke; choking, still feeling the ghost of the grip about her neck. She didn't bother rousing anyone from the house. She made her way downstairs, perusing the selection of books from the library. In the comfort of her cotton, robe-like wrapper garment, she had settled in to the comfortable embrace of a high-backed, burgundy velvet chair next to the dining area picture window. Reading was the only thing she could think to do to settle her mind. It was disturbing. Where was Ralph? The one she most earnestly depended on, seemed mysteriously absent. She anxiously hoped that someone—anyone—could help her with what to do next.

Everyone around her seemed to be more than amiable with whatever she might need, but nothing much beyond that, so the rose was an interesting distraction. She picked up the stem and lifted the bloom to her nose. Curious. It appeared to have no fragrance.

Anna arrived with tea, setting the tray on the opposite side of her table.

"Oh," she said as she noted the bloom. "A white rose. How nice…"

Catheryn blinked, uncomprehendingly. "Where did it come from?"

Anna only gave a mild shrug. "I don't know, but it looks as if someone must owe you an apology."

"Why do you say that?"

"That's what white roses mean," she said, matter-of-factly. "Surely, you must know that."

She had to admit; she didn't know that. She had heard of the language of flowers, but she was not familiar with the various meanings. She picked up the bloom and studied it. As she did so, she realized another person beyond that vantage point; someone standing in the door frame leading to the entryway.

It was a tall gentleman of lean build with short dark hair and a moustache that she didn't readily recognize. He wore a white standing collar shirt and a black double-breasted jacquard vest. The outfit was completed with a pair of black trousers and brogans. Her notice of him seemed to give him the permission he needed to approach, and as he came more in to the light, she caught her breath.

Charlie Danforth came to stand before her, his fingers coming to rest on the table. If the wardrobe wasn't peculiar enough, his dark eyes were downcast in a submissive manner that was different than she was accustomed to.

He cast a sheepish, lopsided grin downward as he raised his hand to finger the lapels of his vest.

"I've been told my militaristic look was a bit...off-putting," he muttered.

She chuckled, as she found the courage to meet his gaze. "I see."

He presented his elbow toward her. "Would you like a stroll to the veranda?"

His formal presentation gave her pause—along with the idea that the house had *ever* had a 'veranda'.

"I understand if you would rather have a chaperone."

Catheryn stifled a chuckle as she exchanged looks with Anna. The attendant smiled with a shy, downward glance and, without a word, lifted the tray on her way toward the kitchen. Casting a subtle glance over her shoulder, in the off-chance that Catheryn may stop her, Anna continued on through the swinging door. It was obvious by the actions of her female companion that the therapist was adult enough to make that decision on her own.

Catheryn raised from the chair accepting the arm offered her. Such formality was not something she was accustomed to, but she took it. She was a long way from home. She knew if she was going to be a stranger in a strange land, she'd best make friends with the natives.

And he was hardly a stranger.

He produced a black slouch hat from beneath his arm and smoothly placed it atop of his head as they walked in silence down the front stairs of the house and into the comfortable early morning sun. The bustling of the day seemed to move about them; other beings moved along the dirt road on their way toward whatever business they might have. She, literally, felt as if she had stepped back in to the eighteen hundreds. The ladies were dressed in their cotton day dresses; their bonnets dressed out in brightly-colored silk ribbon. Shopping baskets of tightly-woven wicker were draped over meticulously-covered arms to ward off sun from the skin. The crinolines beneath their voluminous skirts helped lift the hems from the muddy road, but the ladies still hefted the fabric a touch further with the aid of gloved hands. Catheryn couldn't help but feel, woefully, underdressed, yet, no one seemed to pay the couple any mind. The wooden planks of the walkway presented the way to numerous shops and businesses—the bank, general store, the blacksmith. A wagon, drawn by grey draft horses, rolled along the street, and Danforth was quick to position her to the opposite side of himself, away from the main thoroughfare. If anyone else had moved her so forcefully, she may have objected, but recognizing the chivalrous act for what it was, it did not bother her. It was the *other* thing she noted.

She could feel his touch.

His touch seemed to linger at her waist long enough to draw her eyes to meet his.

"Apologies," he muttered softly, his gaze reluctantly meeting hers. "The mud."

The connection of his gaze with hers, alongside the physical connection, sent a jolt through her body that she hadn't expected. His hand was slow to release her waist.

She swallowed a hard lump forming in her throat, her green eyes dropping to the boardwalk.

"Thank you," she murmured to the weathered floorboards. "I appreciate the air. It was getting a bit...*stuffy* in there."

"The house," he muttered in the direction of the air in front of them. "They mean well."

"I know," she replied. "I...just don't understand where I am."

His eyes snapped back to hers. "You don't remember?"

She didn't expect him to raise his hand—to touch her cheek—but when he did...

She felt herself suddenly whisked away from her pleasant surroundings. There was the squeal of tires against pavement. The crunch of twisting metal. The shriek that took her a moment to realize it was her own voice...

She blinked, in shock. The realization jolted her. Her breath was coming in ragged gasps, and Danforth lurched forward to grasp her shoulders to steady her. She swallowed hard, her eyes meeting his once more, but this time, her pale green eyes were wide with alarm.

"Ok..." she breathed. "I really need to know now. Where... Where am I?"

The teacup in Catheryn's hand chattered against the fine porcelain of the teacup saucer. It was enough to cause Anna to reach out to steady the object in her grasp; not so much to protect the porcelain but from spilling the hot contents down in to Catheryn's lap.

The doe eyes connected with the young medium's gaze as she helped settle the shaking China in the unsettled woman's grip.

"I'm sure it must come as quite a shock, Ms. Catheryn," the young woman offered. "Are you sure I can't get you anything else…biscuits, perhaps?"

The idea of 'biscuits' fixing anything about this almost made Catheryn laugh out loud. The last thing Catheryn could think of was food at a time like this. Her eyes shifted away from her assistant to find Charlie Danforth hovering above her, his expression deeply concerned.

"Am…I…" The therapist couldn't find the words to say it. "I…"

Anna took both of her hands that were clenching the China saucer, grateful to feel the older woman's grip relax.

"No," Anna breathed, assuredly. "No…not…"

The younger woman paused, her brown eyes rose to meet Danforth's, uncertain whether to finish the sentence.

"No," Danforth concluded, abruptly, but softly. "You are still among the Living."

Catheryn exhaled a breath she hadn't realized she had been holding.

"For now, anyway."

The therapist's aventurine green eyes shot up to meet Danforth's, and the shadow of an apology seemed to dance across his features once more. She swallowed hard, hoping to ease her tightening throat with a sip of tea. She struggled to regain her composure, gingerly sipping from the cup before settling it back upon its saucer.

"So…I'm in between."

The young girl across from her could find no words. She could only look to the captain for advice on how to answer.

The therapist blinked; her mouth opening and closing. For someone used to walking people through very emotional situations, she was having a hard time finding her own words. When her green gaze came up, she noted Anna's expression etched with concern.

"Is there anything I can do for you, Ms. Catheryn?"

After a moment's reflection, the uncomfortable woman simply shook her head, her eyes raising to meet Danforth's. She found him watching her closely.

"Could you give us a moment, please, Anna," Catheryn whispered, her gaze not leaving his, making it clear that *he* was to stay.

The woman smiled, seemingly half-relieved that she could leave this difficult situation. Wiping her hands on her white pinner-style apron, she rose from her wooden chair and retreated in to the kitchen.

"Are you alright?" the captain asked, gently.

She blinked, looking up in to his eyes. She felt vulnerable. She knew that. But he was the greatest source of strength she had right now.

"Please don't leave," she said, her eyes pleading.

He paused, but then, chose to take the open seat next to her. He stiffened, somewhat, as she leaned in to his side, but accepted her head against his shoulder.

"So…" she muttered, her gaze shifting off in to the dining area, but her mind was far from that. "This…is Heaven?"

"*Our* Heaven," he replied, directing his correction out toward the room. "Our collective interpretation of it, anyhow."

She found her ability to smile at that.

"I would have expected it to be…a little more…extravagant."

His eyebrows raised at the contemplation. "It was an idea of "Heaven" we agreed to—no illness, no war, no famine…a single thought in this area of the Universe is powerful. We can have anything. We can *create* anything—but a collection of thought in agreement with one another—is more powerful."

"Hence…*this*," she concluded, her smile a touch more present.

"As long as it meets the agreement of the collective."

"What if it doesn't?"

"It's not as solid. Stable."

She found her touch lingering on the cuff of his white cotton shirt, still a bit bewildered how she could feel it at all.

"Is that why I can feel…this?" she whispered, her fingers skimming down the fabric to find the warmth of his hand. "Because… you want me to?"

His eyes met hers, a conflict of emotions reflected back at her. A longing. A resistance to that longing. But he did not look away.

"You don't understand," he said, hoarsely.

Abruptly, he disengaged from her touch. He rose and, briskly, walked from the room.

The pain from his immediate departure tore at her, threatening to move her to tears. She was stressed enough, and his erratic behavior was beginning to push her over the edge.

She sat in silence with her tea. Alone. Again. And more confused now than ever.

13

Surgical Care Unit, University Hospitals, Iowa City, Iowa, USA

Andrew couldn't have been any more shocked when he responded to the knock at the hospital room door.

"Someone called?" the tall, lithe figure greeted, his magnificent blue-green eyes outshining the dullness of the boxy white physician's coat that he wore.

Baldwin did everything he could in his power not to blow his cool.

"Where...have...you...been!" the real estate agent bit out, ushering in the new arrival with a firm grip on his elbow.

The cloaked celestial gazed down at the man in mock admonishment. "Is that the way to greet a friend? After all," the tall being muttered, gazing over the younger man's shoulder toward the pastor, "...you did summon me."

The pastor's hazel eyes grew in amazement, following the "doctor" as he swept in to the room. There was no question that the pastor was well aware of exactly what kind of *help* had arrived.

David Faustus shook off his drowsy disposition, completely oblivious to the awe in which the other two treated the new arrival.

"Ah, Doctor! So glad to catch up with you," the senior therapist addressed cordially, shaking the taller man's hand. "I'm Doctor Faustus—"

"Dr. Santangelo. Yes," the doctor named Ralph concluded, abruptly. "I *do* believe we've met. And, how is our patient doing this morning?"

Ralph edged past the crowd to take the vacant seat next to the bed of the unmoving Catheryn. As he gazed down in to his charge's damaged face, Ralph couldn't help but be moved by compassion. He brushed a strand of her auburn hair out of her face and behind her ear.

"You should have listened," he whispered to her, quietly.

Andrew slid in to the seat, opposite of the masquerading ethereal being.

"It's about time you got here!" Andrew whispered harshly, trying best to convey his desperation without being heard by the others. "We've been under attack here. Nothing we've been doing is working!"

The being's eyes couldn't be moved from Catheryn's sleeping face, stroking the scars that adorned her forehead. "Your concern is noted, but you have to realize not all is within our control."

"What?!" Andrew spit out, leaning closer to him in frustration. "What do you mean not 'within our control'?! I thought you were supposed to perform miracles and some shit!"

Ralph's serene gaze rose to meet Andrew's anxious expression, completely unaffected.

"I am more than capable of performing 'miracles and some shit' but they have to be because she *wants* me to." The elevated being seemed to read the agent's frustration without words. "It's her life. Her decision. I've seen the human will act like steel against pure evil—and win—because it's that powerful, but they have to *want* to fight. I can help, but the lion's share of this is her *wanting* to come back."

"I don't get it," Andrew muttered, shaking his head in frustration. "Why wouldn't she want to come back?"

Ralph's eyes rose to meet Andrew's gaze with sternness behind his dazzling blue-green eyes. "She could be somewhere she doesn't want to leave."

"She's right here!" Andrew insisted, growing more animated by the moment.

Ralph looked down at her, his face etched with concern. "But her Consciousness is not."

The pastor was beginning to take interest in the conversation, leaning over Andrew's shoulder.

"You don't know *where* she is," the pastor murmured. It was more of a statement than a question.

"I have an idea," the guide said, his expression a touch defeated. "But I am forbidden to interfere at this point. As her guide in this life, I could counsel her, but as for where she is *now*…it is her choice."

"But, she's still here," Andrew insisted. "She's still breathing. She's still *in that bed*. She obviously hasn't made her choice yet."

"No, she has not," Ralph agreed, smoothing out the edges of Catheryn's comforter.

"So, that thing out there…" the pastor muttered, leaving the sentence hang as all eyes turned to the senior being in the room.

Ralph released a tight-lipped sigh.

"I might be able to help you with that."

Andrew Baldwin leaned over the cold metal railing of the hospital bed; grateful, for once, not to be the bait for the evening's affairs. He rested his chin on his folded hands that occupied the railing, staring at Catheryn's placid face.

"Catheryn," he muttered, his whisper heartfelt. "You have no idea how you are needed back here. If I understand your 'friend' over there…he seems to think you might need some convincing."

"I wish I'd told you before now. I mean, that house…" He found himself chuckling at the memory. "That house was crazy. I'd never been more scared of anything in my life. But you know…I wouldn't trade that experience for anything in the world. Is that weird? I mean…"

The agent reasserted his grip on the rail. "Everything up to this point has been nothing other than profit and loss statements. Wholesale. Retail. Percentage points…" Andrew sighed. "You made me realize there's more than that. *People* mean more than that—Living or Dead. You don't know how strong you are until you're tested. People can go their whole lives without that. Playing it safe. Demanding that they *know* what they know, but never really…"

He shook his head in frustration, his voice choking, on the verge of tears.

"What kind of life is that? And I *did that!* I don't know if I could have done the things I'd done if you hadn't been there. And if you did that for *me*…It's a lonely world out there; you know that more than any of us. People like us—who hear what we do and see what we do—we need to know that we're not alone. Who else is gonna listen to us? Who else…is gonna understand? I guess what I'm trying to say is…I need you. We *all* need you."

Andrew took a steadying breath, gazing longingly in to the face of the only person in this world that he could honestly call 'friend'.

"What I'm saying is…," he whispered, his voice breaking with emotion. "Come back to us."

"Andrew…" the unearthly voice of calm sereneness called from over the younger man's shoulder. "It's time."

"Time to test those limits again," Baldwin whispered, pulling himself up to his feet. "Wish you were here. Could need a pep talk about now."

He turned to spare a singular glance at the tall, ethereal being next to him as they headed for the hall.

Andrew's hazel eyes, fell, sheepishly to the taupe industrial tile floor. "You think she heard me?"

Ralph smiled warmly, raising a hand to clap him on the back.

"Perhaps."

The ethereal being allowed the younger man to pass through the door frame ahead of him. It was best that Baldwin did not see, especially going in to battle as they were, the doubt that disturbed his serene expression.

14

Catheryn stepped out on to the front platform before the double door entryway of the house. Unlike the cement steps in her world, these steps were the familiar ash-gray barnwood. Of course, she thought to herself. Cement would not have been familiar to their generation.

She had finally found it within herself to exchange the comfort of her cotton robe-style wrapper for a cotton green and white-striped plaid day dress. It was nothing fancy. It had a plain white collar to protect the neckline stitching, as well as white cuffs at the wrists to protect the hemming at the buttoned sleeves. Practicality. That was what this era was about.

She had fussed enough with her auburn hair to pull it back in to a low bun, electing for the center part atop her head. She was learning to blend in a bit. However, she had opted to skip the heavy cage beneath the skirt, in exchange for starched petticoats. It was too late in the evening to worry about being seen by anyone other than the chirping crickets and occasional croaking of the random frogs congregating at the banks of the Des Moines River.

Yes, apparently, the river still existed in this version of "Heaven", and she could hardly blame them. The churning water was less of a roar and more of a gurgling in this creation of bliss. The iron truss pedestrian bridge, had apparently also made the cut in to this iteration of reality. Sparse lanterns lined the floorboards across the bridge's expanse; the light complimented by the sliver moon high in the night sky. Other lanterns lit the boardwalks; hanging from the tin-covered overhang protecting the woodwork. Many of the lamps were beginning to be turned down as many turned in for the night, giving the boardwalk a saffron glow.

Turning in for the night. Catheryn had to chuckle to herself. It was interesting to see that the cycle of day and night still had a place in this version of their Universe, but it agreed with her. She was still very much attached to the Circadian rhythm of the Living world, and she found the familiarity of sleep and awake less…disturbing.

It was beautiful out here.

"Yes, it is."

She smiled. She didn't need to turn to see who the tenor voice was, and it took no guessing as to what the voice was alluding to. It was beginning not to startle her any more to have people suddenly *appearing* in her presence, and she was rapidly coming to realization that thoughts were rarely things kept to oneself here.

After all, as she was beginning to learn—in this realm, thoughts were tangible things.

Catheryn found it within her to address Charlie Danforth with a smile, even though his abrupt departure still weighed heavily in her mind. She was grateful for the company.

He still remained in his black jacquard double-breasted vest. Even though she thought the uniform well-suited for him, this lack of formality was beginning to grow on her.

"Would you care for a stroll?" he proposed, offering her his arm.

She paused, concerned about a repeat of this morning's turmoil.

He re-offered the arm, but not forcing it on her.

"Please," he said, softly. "Allow me to explain."

She sighed, resignedly, but not dramatically. If there was anything she needed right now, for all that had happened since she had arrived, it was an explanation. She took his arm.

The gravel of the main street crunched beneath the hard leather soles of their shoes as they made their way toward the entrance on to the bridge. The warm glow of the lanterns was inviting enough, but she found herself stopping short of stepping on to the barnwood planking, in spite of herself. Intruding memories of the dark and brooding energy from the bridge in her reality came flooding back to her.

"The Darkness does not exist here," the captain explained. "*Feel* for yourself."

It was the first time she had stretched out with her abilities in this environment, and as she did so, she felt nothing but...*nothing.* There were no warning bells. No alarms in the back of her head. However, as she stretched her senses *beyond* the bridge, that feeling was more than alien. He could read her discomfort.

"The collective reality doesn't extend beyond the bridge," he explained. "Beyond that, things get a bit more...muddled."

It made sense to Catheryn. Many of the people from his generation would likely not have travelled more than twenty miles outside of their homes. The railway was just coming in to popularity, so a reality outside of the town limits would be hard to...*collectively* imagine. The world was so much larger to her, but her time was different. She was so lost in her own thoughts that it took Danforth taking her hands in to his own to bring her back. His expression was more solemn.

"Your guide...Ralph," he said, choosing his words carefully. "He showed me things. Things as they are. Things as they *will* be. There's a reason I had to stay away."

His thumbs seemed to stroke over the soft skin on the back of her hands, almost as if to smooth over the effect of what he had to say. She was becoming somewhat alarmed.

"What..." she said, softly but reluctantly. "What did he show you?"

He found himself unable to meet her gaze, and she could tell he was having difficulty forming the words.

"Your destruction."

She pulled back from him, forcing him to release her. Her eyes were large, incredulous.

"How could it possibly...How..."

"If I followed you in to your world, such as I am...there are things," he explained, earnestly, his eyes glazing as the words continued to come slowly. "Things that would follow me."

Fear began to well up within her. The experiences at Bramden House were terrifying enough, but it hadn't phased him. He had bravely seen through it all without barely a flinch. But this...She could tell by his demeanor that whatever Ralph had shown him had truly affected him.

"In every instance. In every eventual reality…" he said, desperate to keep the emotion from his voice. "It was all my fault."

Tears welled up in her eyes. It felt as if her heart was being wrenched from her chest. How could this be? How could Ralph let it be this way?

It was then that she remembered; Ralph's last words to her about coming to see him. About coming down to the house. Desperate for her to change her mind. Ralph knew. Ralph knew all of it.

"No," she moaned, tears spilling down her cheeks. "You could never do that. You could never hurt me."

"I would *never* hurt you!" Charlie Danforth ground out, taking her face in his hands, moisture seeping from his dark eyes as he stared intently in to hers. "But you being around me *will*. Don't you see—you have to stay as far away from me as you can."

She flung herself in to his arms. He held her. Even as she beat at him with her fists, he held fast.

He pressed his cheek against her amber hair, desperately clinging to her as she shook in wracking sobs.

"You know how I feel about you," he muttered, stroking her hair. "I couldn't hide it if I tried. You've touched my existence in a way I had no right to expect. But…you can't stay here."

He drew back to take her tear-streaked face in to his hands once more. "You have to go back."

The "Lilies of Quebec" was the tune that floated down from the dining area, with the illustrious James McCreary, on fiddle and Lillian Marlan on guitar. It was a full dance floor; the entire town showing up for Catheryn's "Welcome" party.

Although, Catheryn was not feeling entirely 'welcome'.

She sat in the far corner of the dining area as the dancers glided by with beautiful silk skirts and luxurious wool frock coats floating by her seated position by the picture window. She was finding her rhythm in this place. Realizing that she didn't need to 'borrow' clothing from anyone; she, simply *wished* it in to existence.

Her ball gown was of gratuitous silk in gold and dark amber stripe. A waterfall of generous lace hung at her open neckline in a breathtaking bertha, matching the trim at the high sleeves near the shoulder. But, without it moving across the floor, the beautiful dress seemed like such a waste.

She placed a white, doe-skin gloved hand to her neck to stabilize the seed pearl necklace. Still no sign of the captain, but there were a generous number of well-wishers taking the floor and flooding the hallways to the outside. She could only imagine this place being full like this every weekend.

If only she could take part in it.

A white, gauntleted hand presented in front of her eyes, and she glanced up, startled.

Standing before her was a gentleman dressed in gray wool, and a frock coat lined in generous gold brocade at the cuffs and standing collar. Her gaze didn't need to travel past the cleanly-shaved jaw and charming grin full of Southern charm to know she was addressing Lieutenant William Moore.

The smile illuminated his blue eyes; his wavy blonde locks still the non-regulation length about the collar.

"May I have this dance, Ms. Catheryn?"

She returned his inviting smile, aventurine green eyes sparkling.

"I would be delighted."

She gingerly took his gauntleted hand, and he swept her, gently, into the frame of the waltz.

"Bill, it's a pleasure to see you again," she smiled, her eyes aglow. "How did you know—"

"Oh, word spreads fast around here, Ms. Catheryn," he answered, smiling warmly. "You look well, although…I am surprised to see you back quite so soon."

"Not…quite by choice," she muttered, unable to meet his gaze for that moment.

"Are you sure?"

She found his gaze, measuring its meaning. It was apparent he was aware of more than she knew.

"Regardless of the circumstance," he continued, intending to push that awkwardness aside. "It is a pleasure to see you, again."

She couldn't help but smile. It was difficult to ignore that Southern charm.

A dark auburn head of hair appeared at William's shoulder, a playful smile raising dimpled cheeks sprinkled with freckles; large brown eyes all aglow.

"Do I have something to be jealous of, William?" the young girl's voice said, whimsically.

Catheryn's eyes grew wide. "Bridgette?!"

The young woman threw herself in to Catheryn's surprised arms. The medium drew back to take in the young woman in front of her. She was no more a child of fourteen; she had blossomed in to the flower of full womanhood, her long silk gown striped of slate blue and robin's egg. The white blossoms of Wisteria formed a crown along her braids of auburn brown, and there was no mistaking the degree of affection on how she took

William's arm.

"Really?" Catheryn beamed, taking the young couple in. "You look wonderful together."

"Who would have thought my type would be a Southern gentleman," Bridgette muttered warmly, gazing up in to her partner's eyes of blue.

The young medium took a mock moment of consideration, before laughing.

"I think it suits you," she said, winking at them.

Bridgette paused, something drawing her attention over her shoulder. A new presence had entered the room, and she didn't need to turn to see who it was.

The younger woman arched a playful eyebrow as she returned her attention to the guest of honor.

"I think someone has just arrived for you," she said, with a hint of a knowing smile. "I think we shall take our leave."

Catheryn grounded herself, unsure how to take the new arrival coming toward her. Charles Danforth was dressed in a fine gentleman's frock coat; his underlying silk jacquard vest one of red with black thread running throughout. The dark waves of his hair were dressed with honeysuckle cream; his thick moustache and heavy brow neatly trimmed. A black cravat was tied at the standing collar of his white bib shirt. It was a look she was not at all accustomed to see on him.

He offered his best presentation of a bow; doing his best not to be overdramatic.

"You are here," she muttered, her voice devoid of emotion; her eyes downcast. "I was certain you'd stay away."

His white cotton-gloved hands were folded, awkwardly before him as his dark gaze looked anywhere but hers.

"It appears all I seem to do is apologize to you," he replied. "I don't mean to."

"It's obvious there is more you are not telling me."

"I know I've been secretive, but let me explain." Reluctantly, as if knowing she could refuse, he offered his gloved hand to her. "Would you take the night air with me?"

She paused, to consider a moment, her gaze sweeping the audience around her. They all seemed capable of entertaining themselves without her.

She took his hand.

"Alright," she muttered.

They stepped out on to the landing, the lantern casting a soft glow upon the wooden steps. She gazed out in to the pink and purple hues of the fading day, the stars beginning to punch holes in to the darkness slowly taking over the sky. She did not miss the electric lights out here. The natural lighting seemed to paint everything in a brilliant rich palette without the interruption of man-made falsity. As beautiful as it was, she couldn't let it distract her. She turned to him. She had to say her peace. She couldn't allow him to keep treating her in this way.

Seeing her ire coming, he raised a hand to her cheek, touching it gently in an attempt to hold her temper in check.

"Everything I do—everything I have *ever* done—was to keep you safe," he whispered, heartfelt. "Even if it was from myself."

"You could *never* hurt me—"

His fingers shifted to her lips.

"Never intentionally," he corrected, his dark eyes pleading for understanding. "Even though…It is still painful to have you angry with me."

She could feel him even though steps away. Everything he said was true. She felt the struggle within him to keep the balance of control. And the magnetic pull of it all was undeniable.

She moved close to him. He allowed her cheek against his chest, her head in the nook beneath his chin as he pulled her close.

15

Surgical Care Unit, University Hospitals, Iowa City, Iowa, USA

Andrew Baldwin let out a heavy sigh as he traveled the darkened corridors, glowing in a deep crimson red light of the hospital basement. Why the lights were red, he had no clue, but it only lengthened the shadows considerably and gave the atmosphere more *ookiness* than it really required. Ralph, still dressed in his impostor white coat, penetrated the shadows with a flashlight so large that it could probably knock out a security guard if they came across one. As it was, Ralph was able to get them past security with his fake credentials. It was unclear if the credentials were that impressive, or if the guard was manipulated by the celestial guide's equivalency to the jedi mind trick. Since no alarms were blaring and no one was chasing them with guns, the young real estate agent didn't care.

"What are we doing down here?" Baldwin anxiously whispered.

Baldwin wasn't sure what a full voice would awaken in the depths of the dungeon-like basement, but he felt it best not to tempt fate. It was clear that the higher being had no such concerns.

"Entities of this density tend to hide out in areas where other people *aren't*," Ralph counseled at a louder volume than Baldwin cared for. "They thrive on stealth."

"And how do we sneak up on them being so loud?" Andrew countered, quietly.

The guide seemed to consider that for a moment.

"Quite right."

Baldwin rolled his hazel eyes, frustratedly. Far be it from himself to be the voice of reason in this situation, but it was rapidly looking as if he were.

Or, perhaps he had more of a mortal experience to fear losing than the ethereal being. He chose not to consider that and pushed forward behind the folds of his immortal partner's white doctor's coat.

"What is down here, anyway?" the young mortal inquired.

"The morgue."

It was everything Baldwin could do *not* to turn around.

"Rumor has it that scientists used to carry out parapsychology experiments down here in the old days," Ralph continued.

"Next to the *morgue*," Andrew concluded, sardonically. "Fine place for that!"

"Well, they had to do it *somewhere*."

It was at that exact moment that a familiar shriek echoed down the ceramic tile hall directly ahead of them.

"That sounds familiar!" Andrew stated, hugging the white fabric of the doctor's coat. "Right around the corner. Don't worry...I'm *right* behind you!"

The celestial being only offered a disappointed smirk as he continued ahead; the light of the flashlight slicing its way through the dim corridor.

As they rounded the bend, there it was; the voluminous black cloud roiling and writhing directly before them. The howl it emitted was ear-splitting. Ralph merely winced, but Andrew reacted more strongly. The real estate agent stiffened upright, strongly in the face of adversity.

And ran in the opposite direction.

"Don't!" Ralph implored.

But it was too late. The amorphous form swept around the immortal being and charged right for the mortal who was making surprisingly good speed considering the dim light.

"HEY!"

Both individuals were given pause by the startling female voice bouncing off the tiled hallway. Backlit by the reddish glow of the emergency generator lights was a thin, waifish form situated between Ralph and Andrew, dressed in what appeared to be a twenties-style sheath dress. She stepped forward in to the dim light, giving more definition to the short bob haircut. The red light gave her rouge red lips an almost black appearance. Her dark eyes glared at the black cloud with a menace that made both men shudder.

"You leave my boyfriend alone!"

The black mass recoiled under the onslaught of the new arrival's emotional outburst, and it was all the distraction that Ralph needed.

The guide's lips seemed to move but with no utterance coming forth. Ralph's hand plunged outward, palm out, and as he did so, the entire corridor erupted in daylight. The dark menace let out another ear-splitting shriek but immediately, began to reduce in size. All parties covered their ears as the black mass continued to shrink down in size, obviously affected by the light glaring forth by the ethereal being before it. Reduced to nothing more than a small ball, the thing continued to disintegrate until it finally disappeared with a pitiful *squeak*, much to the relief of everyone's hearing.

Andrew just stared, open-mouthed as Ralph blithely appeared to brush some contaminated remnants from his white lab coat.

Baldwin glared at the supreme being, looking more than just slightly indignant. "You couldn't have just…*started* with that?!"

"Well, you seemed so proud a yourself when you thought I moved on that I didn't wanna ruin it for ya!" the female flapper spirit explained in her squeaky Bronx accent as the trio ascended the basement stairs.

Andrew was less than amused. "So, you're *not* 'moved on'?"

The waifish entity gave him a playful shove. "Well, of course I am, silly. I'm with *you!* Certainly better than the last mook I was with!"

"Amateurs," Ralph muttered, walking past them, not willing to take any further part in the discussion.

Andrew scrambled to catch up with the guide. "Wait a minute—you gotta help me with this!"

The elevated being did not break stride.

"You are most certainly *not* my charge," the guide countered. "And there are some messes you cause that you are *explicitly* required to clean up *yourself!*"

Andrew pulled up short, a pained expression on his face just as his new-found companion caught up with him. The girl's porcelain doll-like face screwed up in disgust as she gave him another playful shove.

"Whattsa matta?" she squeaked, sharply. "You got another girl or somethin'?"

Andrew stayed silent as they entered Catheryn's hospital room. Faustus stood up from his chair as the team returned, his expression one of expectance as he moved toward Ralph.

"See?" the spectral gal snorted at Baldwin. "That's a real gentleman. He stands when a lady enters a room."

"So, is it over?" Faustus asked.

"Yes," the counterfeit Dr. Santangelo sighed. "I don't think we have to worry about that anymore."

"How did you manage that?"

Ralph had to pause a moment as both Pastor Daniel and Andrew Baldwin awaited his explanation with baited breath.

"New technology," Ralph answered quickly. "The white paper is on the verge of being published."

Faustus arched a curious eyebrow "Oh, can't wait to read it."

16

The morning was beautiful; the white clouds white and fluffy with no sign of rain. As Catheryn stood on the wooden landing at the front door steps, she wondered if "the collective"—as Charlie put it—simply decided on the weather to be like this every day.

She wiped her hands off on her white pinner apron attached to her white and green plaid day dress. She had just finished helping Anna and the others serve breakfast and clear the dishes away to the kitchen. It always amazed her how many guests the house seemed to have. She remembered the workers telling her that the house had always been a sanctuary, even in its earthly incarnation—when Mr. Bramden owned the inn, it was a stop on the Underground Railroad helping escaped slaves find their way to freedom. The injured American Civil War soldiers knew that their survival rate odds were higher if they could just make it to the house. And now it was a spiritual 'halfway house' for those transitioning to the other side of the Veil.

And, apparently, business was brisk.

Her eyes came to linger on the pedestrian bridge. Something always drew her attention there. Perhaps it was how it loomed at the high point, dominating the town skyline. Perhaps it was how it seemed to lead right up to the front steps of the house. And now it was made even more enticing by what Charlie said lay beyond it.

Catheryn was new to this world, but she simply couldn't conceive of a reality dissolving into just...nothing. She had to see it for herself. The structure appeared so innocent, so benign, in the day time. She shielded her eyes from the morning sun, gauging the time from its position in the sky before descending the steps. She probably had an hour or two until lunch prep would start. Looking both ways down the dirt street, she made her way over to the bridge's entrance.

The rustic bridge welcomed her with its normal beckon, but, as she placed her first foot on the barnwood of the bridge structure, something touched her with foreboding. It wasn't loud or overwhelming; just a subtle whisper to stop. At first, Catheryn just felt it was just echoes of past nightmares regarding the bridge in her world. She pressed forward, brushing the warning off.

That was, until she reached the half-way point when the whisper became more of a firm command. Something in her equilibrium seemed slightly off. The bridge felt like it was swaying. She moved over to the wood railing to steady herself, validating the structure was solid. The steel and wood construction seemed perfectly sound. As she continued on, the vertigo got worse. By the time she was at the other end, she barely felt as if she was on firm ground. Was this what "nothing" felt like?

The wooded tree line at her side of the shore looked hazy and cloaked in mist. Perhaps "the collective's" daily forecast wasn't so certain on this side. As her foot touched the opposite bank, she turned to look behind her. She was shocked to find the sunshine of the day had vanished in to a thick fog, following the winding river between her side and the other. She could barely make out that there was any bridge at all.

The shriek that echoed through the wood behind her tore her away from the contemplation; that ear-splitting shriek that had accompanied Catheryn to this reality. The shriek that had been haunting her nightmares, choking off her very life essence. A chill rippled through her and she pivoted in mid-step to turn back to the bridge. She couldn't see the structure at all now. She took a step forward, but what her eyes couldn't see, she couldn't trust. Perhaps she could find another clear fording point down the way.

She shifted and turned to sprint down the shoreline. This was ridiculous.

As she made furtive glances across the water, she became more panicked that she could make out no familiar features there. It was as if the fog had somehow swallowed up the whole town.

The shriek was in pursuit; much closer this time. Nope, it would not catch her. She would not let it. She pushed through the brush and branches that snagged at her cotton dress as she raced away from her pursuer. Dumb. This was a dumb idea. Why did she always let her curiosity get the better of her!

She braved a glance behind her, and she noticed the familiar ragged silhouette darting from shadowy point to shadowy point within the wooded landscape; melting into the darkness, only to reappear closer. Her desperate green eyes turned to find any point to pierce the fog, praying to find some familiar landmark to give her hope.

The ear-splitting cry was so loud this time that it set Catheryn's ears ringing. It so startled her that she lost her footing over a branch which sent her careening, hands first, in to the brush. She flopped on to her back, desperate to triangulate her pursuer to find it a mere ten feet away. The ragged mass of black energetic tentacles rose in to the air, pausing at the lowest branches of the tree, recoiling slightly to find momentum to drive down at her.

That's when the shadow of a thick blade spun through the air and buried itself in to the oak immediately beside the creature. The force of the throw sank the blade up to its bone handle. The creature seemed to reply to the challenge with another shriek, only to have that answered by a second blade landing in to the bark only inches below the last. Rethinking the easy condition of its prey, the creature retreated back in to the woods, melting into the dark shadows from whence it came. The young medium found herself catching her breath, her eyes darting about for the next attack.

Which was why, when the dark leathery hand extended itself down to her, her anxiety sent her scrambling backward. She gazed up in to an intense pair of dark eyes peering back at her from beneath a striped silk turban-like hair wrap. His high cheekbones and hawkish nose screamed of his Native American heritage. His heavy dark doe skin tunic and breeches had seen regular wear but were still in perfectly good condition to shrug off the dirt and moisture of the day.

She took his hand, allowing him to pull her up on to her feet, his eyes meeting hers with a grim expression.

"Not a good hunting day," he said, plainly.

Catheryn only nodded in agreement as he turned down the thin trail from where she had run.

"I'm sorry," she murmured, feeling apologetic in drawing the man out of his way. "I seemed to have lost my way in the fog—"

She didn't even get to finish her sentence as they paused at the bank, looking squarely at the entrance to the missing bridge. Catheryn stared at it, dumbfounded.

"Johnny!" a familiar tenor voice drawled from a point of light on the fogged-in bridge. "Johnny Green! That you?"

Without a word, the warrior gripped the back of Catheryn's shoulder and coaxed her toward the voice as the light melted through in the shape of a lantern. Holding the lantern was the familiar face of Jackson Carter. His gray-green hazel eyes fell hard on Catheryn.

"Found another one, did ya?" the hired hand drawled in his casual way toward Catheryn's savior, Carter's smirk tinged with more than a hint of exasperation.

"You need to keep better track of them," Johnny Green responded, giving the woman a gentle nudge toward Carter. "It's not safe out here."

Carter frowned, his gray-green eyes doubling down on the medium. "She knows that."

"Thank you, Mr. Green," she offered, turning back toward her rescuer. "May I ask what brings *you* out here, then?"

"Hunting," he said, dryly, sliding the last of his long-knives into its beaded sheath. "No competition for it over here."

Without another word, the man turned back, disappearing in to the mists from which they had come. Jackson took Catheryn by the elbow, steering her back to the bridge.

"Ms. Catheryn, I don't know how many lives you think you have left."

"Still working on the one," she muttered, following the man in to the confusing mist.

Catheryn sat before the antique vanity, her gold and brown patterned wrapper over her long white linen night gown. She, absentmindedly, dragged the boar bristle brush through her hair. Staring in to the mirror, her reflection almost seemed alien to her; the flickering light from the chimney of the nearby kerosene lamp dancing over her pale skin and auburn waves. Her mind was light-years away. Anna found her like that.

The young woman appeared over Catheryn's shoulder, dressed in her own brown and gold wrapper for evening; her brown hair dropped down over her shoulder in a long-plaited braid.

"Is there anything I can get you, Ms. Catheryn?"

If Catheryn had it within her to smile at the attendant, she would have. She fingered her auburn strands, admiring Anna's own night-time look.

"Could you help me do that?" the young medium asked, motioning to the girl's braid in the reflection of the mirror.

She offered the guest a slight smile. "Of course."

The two of them sat in silence as Anna separated the hair with the hairbrush. She could see the young girl was watching her, her brown eyes filled with concern, as she segmented out the strands.

"I don't know why I'm here," Catheryn muttered, her face empty of emotion. "Why bring me here if I'm supposed to stay away?"

The girl's doe eyes searched for Catheryn's in the reflection of the mirror.

"You know the house has always been a safe haven, Ms. Catheryn," the woman said, with gentle matter-of-factness. "We would never turn *anyone* away. That's why the captain had you brought here."

Anna watched in the reflection as astonishment rolled across Catheryn's features. The attendant barely had a moment to tie off the braid when the medium pulled away from her. Catheryn's green eyes darted up to physically meet Anna's, as if the reflection was a ruse.

"What did you say?"

Anna's warm brown eyes blinked, not comprehending her mistress's confusion.

"That's why the captain had you brought here…"

"But he didn't," Catheryn corrected, growing more confused by the minute. "Jackson found me."

She was grateful to be looking Anna in the face so she could openly note the girl's growing discomfort.

"But he told Jackson where to find you…"

Catheryn blinked. It made sense. If anyone could find her—find her anywhere across any reality—it would be Danforth.

Charlie.

But if they were to stay away from each other…

The knock at the door disrupted the conversation, and Anna found it a welcome distraction to go answer it. Although the arrival at the door was anti-climactic. Catheryn knew who it was even before Anna opened it.

"Captain…"

Danforth didn't give the girl time to finish. "Thank you, Anna. That is all."

The captain let the girl sweep by him, not moving from his point in the doorway.

"Why?" Catheryn uttered, fixing him with her pale green eyes from across the room. "Why did you bring me here?"

His eyes found the barnwood floor. The antique wallpaper. Anywhere, but her gaze.

"And, don't lie to me this time."

The flickering lamplight seemed to take the darkness away from his eyes, almost giving way to an amber glow. She rose from her chair, and before he could move or utter a word, she pressed her mouth to his. His arms, instinctivey went around her waist, her back; eagerly pressing her to him. The warmth of him was physical, but the energy of his presence also permeating every inch of her being. She surrendered to his will as she felt him inside her mind; bending her control to move against him in the way he only dreamed.

She felt her back pressing in to the mattress of the bed behind her; crying out for him as he pulled the belt of her wrapper from her. His breath was on her neck, the roughness of his moustache and stubble finding the hollow of her throat as she felt him seize possession of her mind. Without a thought, her fingers danced along the buttons of his cotton shirt and jacquard vest, pushing the fabric away to find the dark hair of his chest.

Their interconnected mind was so complete that clothing no longer was a barrier. Any fantasy that sprang to mind, he was instantly a part of, and without a moment's hesitation. She had no recollection when the sheets became wrapped around them, or her body wrapped around his. Her own body moved like a thing apart from her as it appeared to move of its own volition. His mouth was on hers, hungrily, as if either of them needed it to say a word.

Yes! I feel you! she screamed in his mind. *I feel you in my mind. I want you. Take control. I want you to!*

In that moment, something broke. The connection snapped, abruptly. As she came to, she found herself on her back; the sheets around them tangled almost to the point of insanity. She felt him heaving for breath on top of her.

"No, I won't do that!" he gasped. "I can't go there."

As the lustfulness subsided, and her rational mind began to take hold, she realized what had almost happened. She closed her eyes as the shame sunk in. He couldn't do that. He wouldn't do that. It would make him less. Less than the man he was.

Less than human.

"No," he whispered against her ear. "Don't feel that."

His mouth was on hers, again, hot, yet, tender; in a way that was almost toe-curling. It almost made her forget what had almost happened.

Almost.

"This is new to both of us," he muttered, rolling to the side of her and pulling her against him. "We will find our own way through it."

Catheryn awoke to the strange sensation of warmth next to her as the sun streamed through the window. She felt Charlie Danforth move next to her, his Consciousness already stirring. Her fingers rested on the dark hair of his chest, marveling at the texture of it. She glanced up, the darkening stubble of his chin plainly visible. Did he do that, or was she bringing the human out of him? Either way, it made him a damn sexy man.

"I'm glad you think so," he muttered, ceasing to feign sleep as a smile playing across his lips even though his eyes stayed closed.

A laugh rose up in her as she shifted against him, pressing her lips to his own. She drew back, drawing a finger along the stubble of his jaw.

Her expression turned serious as her eyes rose to meet his.

"Are we in trouble?"

A lopsided grin grew on his lips. "You *are* trouble."

"You know what I mean," she whispered, brushing aside his roguish charm. "Not even a day ago, you were demanding I stay away."

She could feel the discomfort stirring between them and she hated to be the one to bring it, but it had to be said. She found his hand beneath the blanket and brought it upward to lace her fingers with his.

"Would the issue still exist if I…I…stayed?"

166

He blinked at her, uncomprehendingly. "Stay. Here?"

"If you followed me in to my world: that was the danger," she muttered, weaving her fingers more tightly with his own. "I could stay here. You said it yourself; we can create any reality we want to here without danger. We can simply...choose it."

She could feel the thoughts churning in his head. Some of the fear diminishing as his eyes lit to that beautiful amber glow. Perhaps, there was a chance.

She began to feel the tantalizing tentacles of his energy weaving through her heart. That feeling would always be there, no matter where she went. They were connected in a way no two ever would be, and that would never leave her.

Nor did she want it to.

His hand found hers under the sheets and he pulled it up to his lips. He kissed the knuckles of her curved fingers tenderly.

"Until you cut the ties...we are bound."

Her eyes closed, and whether it was his will, or some other, she could see it; the cord that stretched from him to her. No matter where they would be, or what happened, it would always be there.

But there was that nagging. What he had told her...

"Your destruction…and it will be my fault."

She pushed the thought aside. No, she didn't want him to think about that now. She didn't want to think about that now.

She just wanted…now. If what he said was true; that a joined reality could create anything, there was a chance.

She closed her eyes and in the comfort of his arms, she willed herself back to sleep.

17

Surgical Care Unit, University Hospitals, Iowa City, Iowa, USA

I feel like I'm in a crazy roleplaying game," Baldwin grumbled from over his cup of coffee. "We've made it through the dungeon. We've slayed the evil goblin…now what do we do?"

Pastor Daniel had just closed out his Sunday morning service and suggested on meeting the team for coffee in the hospital cafeteria. It was a refreshing change to find the holy man in actual modern clothing marking him as a man of the cloth. He sported a short-sleeve gray button-down shirt with the uniform white collar. His charcoal gray wool coat covered the vinyl back of his orange cafeteria chair.

The spirit girl giggled, snuggling in to Andrew Baldwin's side. "I know! Let's go to Puerto Vallarta! Get some sun!"

Pastor Daniel cocked an eyebrow at the young real estate agent, his eyes traveling to the younger man's unearthly companion. "Andrew, do you know you have a—"

"Yes," Baldwin answered, bluntly. "*More* than aware."

"Let me know if you need some help with that," the preacher said, with an unamused frown, leaning back in the vinyl and chrome cafeteria chair.

Andrew wished, desperately, that Ralph was around to hear the clergyman say that.

Faustus frowned distastefully into the cup of less-than-palatable cafeteria coffee. "Well, we need somehow to break through the Veil and reach her."

"There's always prayer," the preacher offered.

Dr. Faustus smiled, gratefully. "There's always that."

Pastor Daniel pressed a finger against his lips.

Faustus arched an inquisitive eyebrow at the holy man. "You have…another thought?"

The pastor shifted his paper collar at his neck as he turned to Andrew. "Andrew, didn't you say you had some experience with lucid dreaming?"

Baldwin frowned thoughtfully. "Once. By complete accident down at the house."

"So, you could do it again, if the circumstances were right."

It was less of a question and more of a statement.

Andrew looked mystified as to what the clergyman meant. "I suppose…but…"

David Faustus perked up, leveling a finger at Pastor Daniel. "I think I know where you're going with this."

"I've not been able to do it myself but I've read enough," the holy man stated, stroking his chin, thoughtfully. "If you get in to a lucid state, you could request to go...anywhere."

Faustus stabbed the simulated wood table top with his finger, a glimmer of hope flashing in his gray eyes. "I've heard studies where dual subjects could enter each other's dream states before."

"Exactly," Daniel said, his gaze shifting back to Andrew. "What do you think? You up for it?"

Andrew's gaze widened. "You want me to enter her...coma? Isn't that...dangerous?"

"We would be here to wake you, so you wouldn't get stuck there," the chaplain, stated, matter-of-factly. "You are in considerably less danger than her. And if you could reach her to convince her to cross..."

"What do you think?" Faustus said, flashing the agent a challenging grin. "You up for it?"

The younger man smirked. "As long as there be no dragons."

The young real estate agent lay in his bed, the city lights outside his window dancing along the ceiling of his hotel room. He had to get in to the rhythm of regular sleep if he was to do lucid dreaming.

And the best way to do that was in a real bed.

Faustus did not begrudge him that and agreed they should probably both find sleep in a place other than an uncomfortable hospital chair. It was pretty clear after their meeting with Catheryn's doctor—her real doctor—that she would not be going anywhere, anytime soon.

Baldwin rolled over and snapped off the bedside lamp. It stayed off for less than a minute before he turned it back on. He could sense a strong presence next to him.

Ralph was seated in the spare upholstered chair to the right of his bed, dressed in linen trousers and a white standing collar shirt. The being feigned a mild look of surprise that Andrew had actually taken notice of him.

"Oh!" the bemused spirit said, casually. "Hello! Did I wake you?"

"Bored without your charge?" Andrew drawled sarcastically, wiping a hand over his tired face.

The blonde-haired agent started, his hazel eyes darting around the room. He seemed almost gleeful at the absence of the painfully constant companion for the last few days.

"Wait! Is she—"

The guide flashed him a bemused smile. "Oh, I sent her shopping. It didn't take much. Just your credit card."

Baldwin's face took on a pained expression.

"Just kidding. I'm suspecting she won't be back for a while, though."

Andrew addressed the guide with pleading hazel eyes. "Couldn't you just take her…you know…the rest of the way?"

"Nope," the being dismissed, with folded arms.

Andrew groaned. "Please, Santa! I've been a really good boy this year…"

"Wrong authority figure…and no, you haven't."

Baldwin collapsed back in to his bed, pulling the sheets up over his head.

"We really should discuss strategy."

Andrew flopped the sheets back down about his waist, staring up at the white ceiling. "So, there *are* dragons."

"Not quite, but…close. Mind fields, to be sure."

"You mean *mine fields*."

"No, I mean *mind* fields. You may wish to take notes. This could get complicated."

The young mortal threw the covers over his face, again.

"Could we do this in the morning?" Baldwin's tired voice managed through the 1,500-thread count cotton sheets.

"No."

"I suppose you're right," the bed's occupant droned.

"Of course, I am," the elevated being chided. "In which way?"

"You're not Santa. Santa would tell me to get in to bed, and go to sleep."

"Don't make me smite you."

Andrew groaned, albeit muffled. The only body part that emerged from beneath the sheet was a flailing hand, in to which Ralph placed a pen and a hotel room pad.

Ralph made himself more comfortable in his chair.

"Try to keep up," the immortal being mused. "Catheryn's life may depend on it."

18

The sun was in the late afternoon position when Catheryn ventured out on to the bridge. She wore her green plaid day dress with a gold and black paisley shawl draped over her shoulders to ward off the chill of the damp breeze rolling over the water. She made it to the midpoint, tipping her face skyward to take in the sun. She felt the light registering on her eyelids but no warmth.

She was pausing to consider why when she felt hands falling on her shoulders.

"Not all senses work the same on this side of the Veil," the strong tenor voice behind her, observed.

Catheryn smiled, turning toward the captain and was surprised to note that he had opted for his military navy blue frock coat this afternoon.

"Official business," he said in response to her thought. "I was accepting a field report from Carter."

She felt a shudder rippled through her, and it was not from the breeze.

"What does he do for you, exactly?"

"My old job."

She turned to address him, directly, drawing the shawl more tightly about her shoulders.

"*He* protects the house?" she queried, more than a touch surprised.

"And a fine job he appears to be doing, too."

"I hear that Peter Elgin is no longer on the premises," Catheryn smirked. "Did he have any role in that?"

She couldn't help but note the play of mock-innocence cross his features and slight smile that alluded to the mischievous.

"Perhaps," he responded, his tone whimsical. "He was only employing your advice."

Catheryn laughed, vaguely remembering her order of non-compliance with ghost hunter commands. Apparently, that was all that it took...with a few other things. She returning her attention to the river behind her. His arms wrapped about her waist, and she let her head fall back against his shoulder. His warmth was most definitely, present, and it permeated her entire being.

"I remember a time when you were on this bridge with me," she mused, her eyes closed to absorb his presence about her. "You offered to leave with me."

"It was before I knew."

She turned in his embrace, gazing up at him with a seriousness that jolted him. "What if I stayed here with you?"

His eyes darted away. "Catheryn, you don't know what you are saying…what you would be giving up. I wouldn't want to be held responsible for that."

"Are you trying to convince me that the warrior now believes in karma?" She sought his gaze, desperately. "Are you trying to say last night meant nothing to you?"

She felt it before he revealed it. She had most definitely provoked his ire, and regretted it, instantly.

He took her in a strong grip about the shoulders, his eyes sharp.

"Last night meant *everything* to me."

She met his gaze with warmth as she touched the swarthy skin of his cheek. "They can't touch us here. We can build what we want. Have the *life* that we want—"

He reasserted his grip on her shoulders.

"But that cost is in exchange for *your* life," he countered, punctuating his statement with a shake. He took a breath to stabilize his emotions. "Your priceless, *human* life. When you come in to this life, it is with a contract; actions you must fulfill, lessons to learn."

She looked up at him, feeling somewhat hurt and betrayed.

"And you can say in the short life you lived that you did that?" she countered.

"I did," he said solemnly. "The rest I learned…after."

It was her turn to take him by the shoulders, the frustration of her previous life fueling her emotions. "And what if I already have? There's nothing back there for me now—"

"You don't know that," he interjected. "If you don't learn it there, you have to learn it here. There's no escaping that commitment. What you are suggesting is akin to…to…"

"Suicide."

The familiar voice behind her startled her, causing her to pull away from Danforth, abruptly. Ironically, she seemed to be the only one surprised at the new arrival.

Andrew Baldwin stood on the bridge only a few paces behind. He had dressed to blend in; wearing a brown tweed suit, vest and brown bowler hat. Even though he blended with the time period, it was his expression of shock mixed with betrayal that affected Catheryn the most.

"You would give up your life? All of us...just to...stay here?"

Catheryn took an unsteady step toward him, still in shock at his sudden appearance.

"Andrew...I...I didn't mean—"

"Do you know what we've been doing trying to save you?" the young man's face a mask of shock and anguish. "To bring you home? While you prefer to live in this...this...fantasy?!"

"Andrew," Danforth interjected, softly. "That's enough—"

"And you!" Andrew delivered sharply, punctuating his statement with a stabbing finger. "Do you know how much suffering you've put her through?"

The officer looked away, unable to meet the haughty gaze of the accusing man.

"Time is nothing for you here but she's gone *months* suffering over you!" Andrew delivered angrily, his hazel eyes brimming with tears.

Catheryn reached toward him. "Andrew, please—"

Andrew Baldwin cringed in pain, grappling with the bowler hat over his head. "Ah..."

The younger man staggered back, nearly tripping over his brown brogans, his expression of agony ripping at Catheryn's very being. She started forward to try and help, but Danforth's arm thrust out before her to stop her, unsure what to make of it himself.

Baldwin seemed to be battling in the grip of some unseen opponent.

"No!" the new arrival cried. "Not now! NOOOO!"

And in a blink, Andrew was gone.

"Damn it!" Baldwin screamed, ripping the black sleep mask from his face, sending his ragged blonde hair in a multitude of directions.

Normally, that would bother him, but the unravelling of the events he had just witnessed, bothered him more.

He sat upright, witnessing the hazel eyes of Pastor Daniel watching him with concern. Ralph chose to stand back in the corner, cloaked in shadow.

"I told you not to get wrapped up in emotion," Pastor Daniel chastised, a supportive hand on the real estate agent's shoulder. "It will snap you directly out of the lucid dream state."

"I wasn't expecting to see *him* there," Baldwin growled, depositing the sleep mask on the bedside table with a frustrated slam.

"Who?"

"Danforth!"

Andrew could see the processing of information flickering across the pastor's face. Long hours in the hospital room provided ample time to catch

180

the preacher up on the happenings back at the house, but it was a lot to track. Even now. But the holy man's expression was not what attracted Baldwin's attention. Although partially cloaked in shadow, Andrew translated it, perfectly.

"You *knew!*" Baldwin shot at him from across the floor.

Ralph's arms were folded, defensively against his lithe form. "Of course, I knew!"

"Then *why!*" Andrew delivered at the guide, brusquely. "Why did you send us in to the realm with her…her…dead boyfriend…and expect her to come back to the Living!"

The preacher blinked. "He's stolen her?"

"No," Ralph ground out, the frantic pacing as he thought, pulling him out of the shadows. The frustration on his face was a sharp contrast from his usual serene state. "He's protecting her."

"All of this," the advance being muttered, his hands fluctuating in the air at some unseen force. "All of these actions were not in the potential reality stream."

It was Andrew's turn to blink, but in sudden realization.

"So, what you're saying is that they've rewritten *fate* here," Baldwin interjected, throwing his hands up to rake his fingers through his hair.

"Great…that's just…great…"

Ralph marched over to Andrew, drilling his downcast expression with his brilliant blue-green eyes. "What I'm saying is that I don't know the outcome of this."

Pastor Daniel's hazel eyes squinted at the tall man. "How could you not…*know?*"

The lithe figure refocused his attention on the preacher. "All beings are blessed—and cursed—with free will. Normally, we have a view that calculates all potential outcomes to a situation, so it could be coaxed, or steered to aid in our charge's development, but…"

Ralph returned to pacing, tapping a strategic finger against his lips. "…she's in a realm that gives her the ability to create her own reality which introduces infinite variables that cannot, easily, be accounted for."

Andrew flailed helpless limbs in the air. "Can't you just pop over there? Break the spell?"

"I'm not really permitted over there…"

Andrew drilled daggers at the being. "You better not be trying to tell me this 'isn't your department'?"

Ralph frowned. "Our guidance is still sought and respected over there, but… 'not my department' does fit, I suppose. Our job is to direct here; on this plane."

Baldwin's frustration was mounting. "But you could go…"

"And how well did that exactly work for you?" the elevated being quipped at a level of sarcasm rare, even for him.

"Actually…" Andrew reflected on the dream state events. "I think I may have been making an impact."

It was turn for Ralph to be given pause.

"I was getting through," the young man recalled. "I just got snapped back before…"

The tall being fixed him to his spot with a slender finger, wheels of thought turning behind those intense blue-green eyes.

"You just need more of a stabilizing influence," Ralph muttered, more to himself than aloud. "I can do that from here. That is permissible."

Pastor Daniel addressed the younger man from over top of his wire-rimmed spectacles. "Can you do it, again?"

Baldwin's expression bordered on incredulous. "I was lucky to do it *now*."

"Time moves at a faster rate than here, which means more can happen the longer we wait," Ralph explained, his expression grim. "We can't wait. We must try, again."

DARCIE McGRATH

19

The tea tray came to rest on the edge of the table next to the picture window without having been requested. Anna only cast Catheryn a sympathetic look before retreating in to the kitchen. The medium decided that if she left the house, Anna might be what she missed the most.

Well, second-most.

Charlie slid in to the vacant chair across from her, still dressed in his uniform. She found the uniform exceedingly attractive, and the benefit of the intuitive collective environment is that she didn't have to tell him that.

He reached across the ruddy cherry tabletop and took her free hand in his own as she gingerly sipped from her tea cup. She could feel his concern from across the table without words.

"Are you alright?" he quested, stroking the back of her hand with his thumb.

She terminated the sip, settling the fine bone china cup on to the saucer.

"Why does it feel like I'm…cheating…somehow?" she muttered down in to the beverage.

He considered her words a moment. "Any challenges, lessons, or contributions you are required to complete will not be forfeit. You would have to complete them here."

She looked down at his hand, and took it into hers.

"And complicate your life," she whispered, looking about the dining area of the house as if searching for something. "I have no place here in this world."

He took her hand and raised it to his lips, kissing the knuckles, affectionately.

"I'd go through Hell for you."

She stared, unblinkingly into his dark eyes. "I think you've already done that."

"Come," the officer invited softly, pulling her up from her seat. "I want to show you something."

The pair ventured down the wooden front steps of the house as dusk was beginning to settle in to the valley, the familiar lavenders and pinks painting the sky. They passed one of the female attendants extending her brass lamplighter up to light the hanging lantern in front of the house doorway. He steered her left down the main road, the gravel crunching under foot as they walked. It was an area of the town she had not really explored at any time during her travels, and she found herself appreciating the mature grove of oak trees that shaded the road. Set back from the road was a single-level log cabin. A lantern lit the rough-hewn gravel walkway up to the front steps that, unlike the Bramden House, were made of reddish brick. Rough-cut timber formed fencing around the perimeter, and floating in a beauty all their own were dancing balls of light, weaving in and out of the trees.

Catheryn's face pinched, quizzically. "Lightning bugs?"

Charlie leaned on the rough wooden crossbeams of the fence, observing the light show.

"Nope," he drawled, casually. "Just fey."

Catheryn's eyes widened at the word. In her psychic world, she had encountered wild, unhuman, natural energies she classified as "elementals". She oftentimes wondered if that was where mankind's earliest spirit tales came from as she noted the tiny balls of light shift and change color, swirling through the dark, completely unafraid of their presence.

"What are they doing here?" she breathed, her green eyes wonderous.

"They live here…" he shrugged, speaking matter-of-factly. "As much as they live anywhere, I suppose. We're in-between dimensions, so they come and go; sometimes they're here, sometime on your side. They like to stay in our trees."

In the fading light of day, she could almost make out shadows, moving through the branches of the tree; like monkeys scurrying from prey. One of the shadows shifted as she watched, and a tiny head seemed to materialize through the foliage. The creature was no larger than a toddler. Its eyes were almost as big as saucers and black as polished onyx. Its skin was tight against its skull and seemed almost a smooth pale gray. Its ears were close along the side of its head and long spindly fingers seemed to part the leaves to get a better look at her. It spat, in a way, that almost reminded her of a cat's hiss, and it retreated into the boughs to cloak itself.

Charlie just chuckled, nonchalantly. "What's *his* problem?"

It was such a cavalier attitude toward something so alien that it made Catheryn laugh. It also made her realize just how much more of this world there was to explore.

He took her by the hand, guiding her up the two steps before pushing the barnwood door inward. The only light from inside the house consisted of a crackling fireplace made of stone. A flat hearth extended from the fire with matching brick similar to the front steps. Cast iron pans hung from a hook next to the fire's opening with numerous cook pots of various sizes hanging within the blazing embers. There was a beautiful oak set of table and chairs before her, drawing her eye to the light turquoise blue milk-painted walls surrounding them. The pantry cupboard was a similar country red that deepened the oak color of the wood.

He retrieved a lantern and brought it over to the table and pulled out a chair for her to sit down.

Catheryn's gaze roved over the intricacies of the cozy cabin when she sat down.

"Whose house is this?" she asked.

"Mine."

He caught the surprise in her eyes as he took his seat at the table.

"A man can't be expected to live in a boarding house forever," he chuckled, his hand gesturing toward the Bramden House. "That's a lifestyle for vagabonds and bachelors."

She smiled, teasingly, her eyes dropping to the table top. "And…you're not those things?"

He smiled his roguish grin. "Somehow, I'm finding less of a future in that."

He pushed away from the table and turned toward the fire. "Would you like some coffee?"

She took in the sparse light from the hand-blown glass window next to the pantry. "I don't think so…"

Her hand brushed against an object on the table. It was a small wooden box that almost blended perfectly with the wood finish of the table top. She picked it up; the object fitting neatly in the palm of her hand.

"What's this?" she asked, working the lid loose.

He looked up from the hearth. "Oh…that."

The matte finish of the box made it difficult to open, but the lid eventually came off. Inside, on top of a cloth, was a gold ring. Inside the setting was a beautiful pea-sized garnet.

Catheryn's breath caught. "It's beautiful!"

He returned to the table without the coffee, reclaiming the chair across from her.

"It belonged to my mother."

It was so simple, yet elegant. She shifted the box to show off the jewel in the sparse light.

She gazed at it, adoringly. "It's lovely."

"I want you to have it."

Catheryn's pale green eyes snapped up to his, the fire light dancing in them showcasing her surprise.

Captain Charlie Danforth reached across the table, claiming one of her hands with his own, his expression earnest.

"You know that I would ask you if I could," he whispered, heartfelt. He gestured to the walls surrounding them with his free hand. "I created this with you in mind. For us. It was a dream."

Catheryn opened her mouth, but the words would not come.

"My mother held my heart for my whole life," he explained, softly, gripping her hand more tightly. "That ring was to go to the woman of my dreams. Whatever happens—however this goes—this belongs to you."

Emotion spilled over her aventurine green eyes in the form of a single tear. There was no doubt in his words. What he said was undoubtedly true and, in this realm, he could not lie.

"Ask me then," she whispered. "Even if it comes to nothing. Ask me anyway."

His dark eyes brimmed with tears as he found the courage to reach for her other hand. There would be no sweeping romantic gesture. No bended knee. It didn't matter. Not now. Not ever.

"Marry me," he uttered, earnestly. "Marry me, Catheryn Greye…if you will have me."

She moved to the other side of the table and he rose to meet her. Her lips were on his before he moved to pull her in to his arms. He kissed her, ardently; her kiss matching his intensity.

"I will have you, Captain Charles Danforth," she replied, drawing back to stroke his cheek. "Come what may."

His dark eyes glowed with the amber glow of intensity, and she caught her breath as he swept her legs from beneath her. She clung to his neck, her mouth on his as they found the fur before the fireplace, beneath them.

And the unbreakable cord between them weaved the magic spell, intertwining them, body and spirit, for the remainder of the night.

20

Comfy Inn and Suites, Iowa City, Iowa, USA

The magic eight ball toy was providing no answers today. Andrew

Baldwin was on the fourth turn of the round device, and it still only gave him

vague nonsense. He never understood what Catheryn saw in the thing.

He placed the device, window-down on the hotel bedside table and

rolled over to stare at the stark-white ceiling. Sleep was very slow in coming,

and even if he was to find her in the quagmire of the in-between state, what

could he tell her to bring her back from the man she loved.

"Trouble sleeping, Andrew."

The owner of the serene voice from the corner of the bedroom stepped

out of the shadows; as if Andrew had to look.

The ethereal being landed in the upholstered chair next to Baldwin's

bed, gazing down at him, sympathetically.

Ralph sighed. "I've been doubly harsh with you. It's put a lot of pressure

on you and that's not fair."

He crossed his legs for better comfort as he leaned closer to his adopted charge.

"And, as a thank you, I helped your lady friend find her way home. She said to thank you but…it really wouldn't have worked out in the end. You're not exactly her type."

The blonde-haired young man finally found something worth chuckling over. He'd never been so happy to be dumped. But after a time, he returned his hazel-eyed stare, unblinkingly to the ceiling.

"How? How do I convince her to come back? I could tell Catheryn all day long how great she is, how I'd miss her, how Dr. Faustus would miss her…or how many people she could potentially help, but…" Baldwin crossed his forearms over both eyes. "I can't tell her what the future holds. I can't tell her life will be better than it is right now…"

Baldwin could feel the energy change in the room without even removing his arms from his eyes. Something in Ralph's demeanor had changed.

"What?" Andrew muttered from his prone, sightless position. "What did I say?

"Andrew," Ralph muttered. "You're brilliant!"

"I thought that was your job."

The immortal being reached out and touched Ralph's shoulder. "You said exactly the right thing. I think you just made this job ten times easier." Ralph smiled as he saw the plan unfold before his vision. "You just need to find her. I'll do the rest. There's one wildcard left, unplayed."

"Do I have to play cards? I hate cards."

"No," he whispered, a smile lighting up his serene expression. "You just have to find her."

Catheryn lay with her cheek on Charlie Danforth's bare chest, staring vacantly out in to the room of the rustic cabin. The sun streamed in the antiquated glass panes, focusing on their bed, as he still slept, blissfully.

The question she had to ask herself was, why wasn't she.

She gazed at the garnet ring on her finger, the gold shining against the nest of dark hair on his chest. It was everything she'd dreamt of.

So, why was gazing at the beautiful ornament filling her with a feeling of such dread.

The newness of being here, and being with him, would wear off over time—she had accepted that, but the churning feeling of lead in the pit of her stomach wasn't that. Something wasn't right about this. She was forgetting something. Something extremely important. And if she didn't come to the realization soon…

"Cold feet?"

She smiled at the sound of his voice. She slid her hand up his chest, drawing upward, her lips only scant inches from his. She marveled as his energy melded with hers, setting the area where her heart resided, aglow. That never would get old. Pressing her lips to his, she reveled in it, allowing herself to *feel* away the unease that had previously pained her.

"What should we do today," she said, her smile a touch mischievous.

"I think…" He seemed to muse over that, playfully before rolling over to pin her in the bed with her wrists next to her head. "We should break in this bed."

She chuckled, her aventurine green eyes aglow. "We did that already."

"We could…do it some more."

She laughed, shrugging him off of her. She retrieved her white dressing wrapper from the bedpost. "I think…I might need some more clothes."

He propped himself up on an elbow, flashing her his famous roguish grin. Another thing she felt would never get old.

"Why Ms. Catheryn. The scandal," he said in mock astonishment. "Are you suggesting you'd move in with me?"

She smiled at him blissfully, wrapping her fingers around the tall bedpost, the sun playing off her ring.

"How quickly does gossip move around here?" she said, playfully.

Bramden House was strangely dark and silent when Catheryn and Charlie entered the next morning. Usually, the house would be at full bustle about now, but the house seemed strangely, vacant. She had just stopped by to collect a few things and return a few loaned clothing articles before returning to the cabin. She wasn't exactly sure how to explain that to everyone, but as she learned, secrets in this town tended not to last long.

"Surprise!"

The entire household emerged from the kitchen. Dr. Coyle was there, along with Jackson Carter, Amelia and a few others from town. Anna headed the jolly crew with a lovely bunt cake and a candle. Catheryn was unsure whether to be happy or mortified.

"News travels fast, Ms. Catheryn!" Anna stated, all smiles as she placed asituation bunt cake on the table. "Congratulations to you and Captain Danforth. Welcome to town!"

Catheryn had finally decided on 'mortified'.

"Oh, no!" Catheryn attempted to interject over the cheers. "I think there's been a misunderstanding—"

Jackson moved forward, taking Catheryn completely by surprise as he lifted her left hand to examine the ring finger. "That's quite a rock you got there, Ms. Catheryn…err, should I say…*Mrs.* Captain Danforth?"

Charlie Danforth seized her arm, sensing her emotional overload. He felt it best to remove her from the situation, quickly, until she could process the well-intentions of the crowd.

He could only chuckle as he steered her in the direction of the secluded entry way. "*Mrs.* Danforth? A word?"

They moved, the jubilant celebration in the next room only growing in intensity as latecomers filed through the back door next to the kitchen. She leaned on the captain, suddenly feeling very woozy. She could feel her heart beating wildly.

Wait. When did that start? She hadn't heard that sound since she had awakened here.

"Andrew?"

Catheryn looked up at the sound of Charlie's voice. Standing there, alone, in the hallway, was Andrew Baldwin. Still dressed in the brown tweed suit and bowler hat as previous, unlike the other celebrants, the young man's face was less than jubilant. She could sense the captain's unease in his reasserted grip on her forearm. And still, above all the din that was growing more muffled in her hearing, was the pounding of her heart.

"Andrew, what are you doing here?" Danforth queried, with a quizzical smile.

"You have to come with me, Catheryn," Andrew said, his face expressionless. "It's important."

Danforth edged his way ahead of Catheryn to place distance between her and the odd visitor.

"Andrew, I don't know what's going on here," the captain stated, blocking any forward progress of the strange arrival by an outstretched hand, in front of them. "Maybe we can go in the parlor and talk about this."

"Catheryn, it's important that I speak to you…"

With that, the young man lurched forward, past Danforth, catching hold of Catheryn's right wrist.

"Now!" Andrew pressured.

Catheryn's vision wheeled, making her nauseous. The celebrating crowd behind her was becoming increasingly muffled. Danforth was at her side, stooping to catch her as her knees went out from under her. Andrew, refusing to let go as Danforth shouted…something. Was it to her? Was it to Baldwin?

And over all the chaos swirling all around her was the constant tattoo of her beating heart.

"Catheryn."

There was the voice, again. That kind, soothing voice that she had been hearing over the last several months. The voice that comforted her and lulled her to sleep. The voice that was there when she was terrified of the dark when she was a child. She knew that voice. Trusted that voice.

"Catheryn, I'm sorry. Please forgive me. I've been exceedingly unfair to Captain Danforth. I showed him the path to a future that was threatening..."

The noises around her continued, but it was more like hearing sound with cotton in her ears. The voices seemed more frantic and urgent now, but the movement around her seemed blurred in shadow. She felt hands lowering her gently to the floor.

"...there are few doors in our lives where the future may be revealed to us. It is important that I share this with you now. It is important that you know..."

The shadows cut out, replaced by images crisp and clear. A jubilant Dr. David Faustus raising a glass, his hair a little grayer around the temples.

"...and to my partner, Dr. Catheryn Greye. May our future be bright ..."

Her body was weightless, the muffled noise of the house becoming more distant.

A brilliant light flashed across her vision. People she didn't know. There was a plaque with her name on it. A man with thinning gray hair and glasses, dressed in a fine windowpane suit was holding a microphone.

"To Dr. Catheryn Greye…for your tireless hours of meritorious service at the Veteran's Hospice Center. Words are not enough…"

It was disorienting. The images were churning. The noise discombobulated, but very clearly, in the background was the sound of her beating heart.

Another brilliant flash, and there was a young girl running to her. She couldn't have been no more than five; her long dark hair cascading over her shoulders, all the giddiness of childhood displayed on her dark complexion. She felt the weight as the child launched in to Catheryn's arms, her warm amber eyes full of light and love.

Those amber eyes that were so familiar.

She couldn't breathe. The light flashed before her vision again, but no more pictures came. Her heartbeat became more maddening, in obvious signs of distress. She flailed out for a handhold, a touch.

But there was nothing. She didn't know where she was. All she knew is she needed air.

DARCIE McGRATH

21

Surgical Care Unit, University Hospitals, Iowa City, Iowa, USA

Catheryn Greye gasped, struggling to remove the space alien attached to her face. A cacophony of noise filled the room with alarms as she felt hands struggle to pin her arms in place. Air rushed in through the apparatus around her nose and mouth, and she ceased struggling. An African American nurse with short hair and pink scrubs was attempting to say something to her, but she couldn't hear it through the ringing in her ears. Another doctor with silver, wire-rimmed glasses hovered above her, his surgical cap still on his head from being yanked in to the room, unexpectedly. He was also trying to talk to her but she still couldn't hear.

She collapsed, exhausted, in to the bed as numerous people whirled around her, but through all of it remained the African American nurse in pink scrubs.

"Can you hear me, Dr. Greye?" she heard the nurse ask, albeit muffled. "I'm Nurse Bonnie. Don't try to talk. Just give me a thumb's up if you can hear me."

Catheryn found that her body would comply with the request. The nurse smiled, brightly.

"That's good! You've been my quietest patient until now, but that's okay," the nurse offered, voice still muffled. "Glad to have you with us!"

Nurse Bonnie was more than attentive for anything she needed, but what she needed was answers, and there was only one living person that could give them to her. Even though the nurse was very reluctant to allow visitors in her weakened state, she knew her female patient wouldn't be at peace until she could have them.

David Faustus entered the room, his charcoal gray window-pane blazer folded over one arm. Still business casual, but his expression was all concern.

"Catheryn," he breathed, sliding in to the chair next to her bed, offering her an awkward hug around all of the tubing and wires about her. "You had us so worried."

"Thank you," she whispered, weakly. "And I don't mean to sound ungrateful, but I need to know—where is Andrew?"

Faustus tried not to feel brushed aside, as he blinked at her, uncomprehendingly. "Andrew, why—"

"I..." Catheryn struggled to recall the exact chain of events. "I was…where I was…and Andrew somehow…pulled me out. Maybe I just dreamed it…"

Faustus' brow knitted in confusion as he pulled out his phone.

"I don't know. He went back to his hotel room to get some sleep," he recalled, putting the phone up to his ear.

Andrew Baldwin caught his breath, slowly backing away to leave more space between himself and Charles Danforth. The captain's temper was a thing of legends, and he feared being on the receiving end of it. Where was Ralph when he needed him?

Charlie was on his knees, staring at the empty barnwood floor before him. He seemed unsteady, bewildered. Catheryn was in his arms, and then something pulled her. He reached out for her with his left. He looked down at his hand. Inside, was a gold band ornamented with a simple garnet.

Baldwin was so focused on the captain that he hadn't realized he'd backed into the far wall when he did. He waited for the officer to lash out; to yell, to rage. But nothing. He watched as the larger man's shoulders fell; his palms coming to rest on the floor. The only thing that seemed to radiate from the man, was sorrow.

"She's gone," he muttered, down at the floorboards.

Andrew felt it through the walls; the tremor rising from the ground. Did he imagine it? He cast his hazel gaze outside the windows lining the front double doors. The people walking the streets outside seemed to give pause. No, they felt it, too.

Danforth drew his left hand up, gazing down at the ring that was still there. He held it in a vicelike grip, raising it to his forehead.

The tremors grew stronger. The people in the next room broke from their air of celebration, their tone casting questions between themselves. If anyone in the vicinity questioned the existence of the tremors before, they didn't now. It was at that moment that Andrew heard the grinding coming from outside.

He gazed outside once more, and he noted the foot traffic that had been casually strolling the main street, was now at a dead run. The stones of the nearby bridge were beginning to flake; dust and debris falling down in to the river below. As the tremors increased, there was an agonizing groan as the metal girders of the bridge began to buckle and sway.

The conversation in the next-door room switched from curious rumblings to shrieks as Andrew witnessed spider cracks beginning to form along the goldenrod-colored walls of the entryway.

But in the middle of the din, Danforth was still; unnmoving in the middle of the floor, clutching the remnants of the one thing he cared about most in the Universe.

The white door leading in to the dining room fell open. Anna emerged, unsteady, as the room continued to shudder and shake. She found Danforth on the floor.

"Captain, where's Ms. Catheryn?" she managed over the din, falling to the space next to him. "Captain, what's wrong?"

"She's gone," a tenor voice of calm sereness, answered from in front of her.

Ralph had somehow blinked to be in between Andrew and the fallen man, dressed in a brown frock coat and red, double-breasted vest. He appeared to be completely oblivious to the chaos around him as he managed, without challenge, to move across the floor to the grief-stricken man.

The ethereal being knelt down; a hand coming to rest on Danforth's shoulder, his blue-green eyes full of compassion.

"His world is, literally, falling apart," Ralph whispered.

Charlie's dark eyes rose to look up at the elevated being; eyes a mixture of rage and grief, tears spilling down his cheeks.

"You took her away," the soldier ground out.

Even with that accusation, the stricken man could only hide his face behind the fist made around the ring he still held.

"No, I didn't." Ralph reasserted his grip on Charlie's shoulder. "She saw a future that you could not. You built this place—a place like no other—as a love letter. To her."

If the guide's voice was to calm him, it only sent him in to a stronger fit of tears. He squeezed his hand even tighter as his grief flowed.

And the tremors became even more severe. People from the dining area panicked as the wall decorations began to fall. A Hoosier cabinet lurched forward and crashed to the ground. The guests rushed past the people in the entryway, meeting outside with others that were beginning to collect there.

"We could have been happy here," Charlie countered, bitterly.

"But not forever," Ralph whispered.

"This world would have been fine for a time," Ralph uttered, quietly, yet firmly. "It was very real for a time, but her world…it's much larger than yours. Such an advocate for her to move forward, but a luxury you refuse to permit for yourself."

The tremors did not let up. White plaster was beginning to crumble down from the ceiling above them. Andrew had felt a semblance of safety in the advanced being's calmness, but that began to slip away as he began to see that demeanor leave the higher being's face.

"Andrew," Ralph stated, his face turning grim. "I'm afraid it might be time for you to take your leave."

Baldwin stared at the guide, incredulously. "We can't just... *leave* him here!"

Andrew opened his mouth to say something when a noise cracked against the floorboards behind them. It came from the space vacated by the party wishers. It almost sounded like a gunshot, but there were three such cracks, in rapid succession.

They all turned to look back and stared up, in astonishment. Dressed in a burgundy sheer dress with a deep V-shaped Peachtree neckline, and long gray hair rolled up in a severe chignon, was Abigale Bramden. She wore her white dress gloves, and in her left hand, she held a walking stick of Irish blackthorn. It was fairly clear to all in the hallway, that it was the origin of the sound that jarred everyone's attention. Even her appearance seemed to startle Danforth enough to cease the tremors.

"That's quite enough, Captain," she delivered, sternly. "Just what do you think you are doing to my house?"

"You're here..." Danforth stammered.

"Of course, I am," she delivered in her usual blunt fashion. "I needed to make sure my heirloom china was being gifted to a worthy bride."

She managed across the debris toward Danforth, not bothering to hide her disappointment in the damage. She stopped just short of him.

Her voice dropped to something of a more intimate whisper, not void of compassion.

"Charlie, this place has been your world long enough. This *world* has been your world long enough. The only difference between you and Catheryn is that she was brave enough to leave it."

Abigale reached down just far enough to lift his chin to look at her, her eyes addressing him with the wisdom of her years.

"You are capable of great things, Charles Danforth," she murmured, her voice unusually calm among the din. "Traveler of dimensions. Builder of worlds. I was proud you have allowed me to serve with you so long. But now it's time for me to take over…and for you to move on."

Charlie looked mystified. "But this is home."

Abigale's chin raised a fraction. "And it always will be."

Ralph drew back to give the two beings some space, finding a spot next to a silent Andrew Baldwin.

"Andrew," the elevated being addressed, his serene calm returning to him. "I think it's time you returned. I need to have a word with our Captain Danforth."

22

Surgical Care Unit, University Hospitals, Iowa City, Iowa, USA

"Andrew!"

Catheryn nearly vaulted out of her bed when the young real estate agent entered the hospital room. Nurse Bonnie made sure to ease her charge back in to bed before the patient did any serious damage to herself.

Catheryn was just happy to be free of the ICU and in a general hospital room. The doctor had been by to check on her and gave the green light to have her discharged in a day or two. She was already in high spirits when Andrew arrived.

Baldwin had eased into a fresh faded blue hoodie and blue jeans for the occasion. He still managed his usual hairstyle but a little lighter on the styling wax. Faustus relinquished his chair next to her so the two could chat.

"I'm so glad you are okay," she said, beaming at him. "I had the most...concerning dream about you."

A certain dread seized the agent. "Oh, you did?"

She blinked, fighting for recollection.

"I was in a dark place…and you pulled me out of it," she muttered, shaking her head. "I didn't see you come back with me."

She chuckled, good-humoredly. "Weird, right?"

Andrew leaned in; his expression curious. "Do you…remember anything else?"

Catheryn seemed to search his face, as if it would help it come back to her.

"I guess…there was a car accident?"

Andrew fell back in to his chair, somewhat bewildered, almost knocking in to Nurse Bonnie as she adjusted Catheryn's fluids bag.

"Yeah," Baldwin muttered. "Right. There's that. A car accident."

"Oh, I hope it wasn't a deer," the nurse interjected, exchanging the bags. "They're awful around here."

"You okay?" the real estate agent asked, searching her eyes for any other sign of remembrance.

"I think so," she said with a smile, a touch more assured. "Would it seem strange to say that I think I'm…*done* with the house for now?"

David Faustus fell back against the hospital wall, his brow knitting in curiosity. "Really?"

"I don't know why, but…" Her gaze seemed to penetrate the walls of the hospital, out to a different trajectory entirely. "I don't think that place holds anything for me anymore."

Andrew just blinked at her, perplexed. So, the memory of everything during her time there. Everything she had done. Everything she had said…

Just. Gone.

"It's better that way."

Andrew startled, turning around to find Ralph's slender form, resting against the far wall of the hospital room, dressed down in a pair of linen trousers and off-white collar shirt.

Baldwin's face was stern, despite the celebratory mood about them. He wasn't at all surprised the being could read his thoughts, but he was surprised that none of the other occupants of the room seemed to take note of him.

"What did you say to him?" Andrew asked.

The ethereal being only flashed Baldwin a secretive smile that set his magnificent blue-green eyes flashing.

"That's between me and my charge."

Baldwin's hazel eyes blinked in confusion. "I thought Catheryn was your charge."

Without a word, or any other indication that there would be any, the spiritual being simply vanished, leaving a mystified Baldwin to return his attention to his companions.

They all settled into a lighter conversation, full of hopeful ideas for the future. So engrossed were they in the pleasure of each other's company that they failed to notice the little girl peeking around the door frame. Her dark complexion and even darker eyes, took in all of the strangers. The vibe of all the personalities in the room made her smile, sending her dark eyes in to an almost amber-like glow.

"Melissa?"

The little girl turned toward the female voice behind her, her long dark braid flipping over her shoulder.

"Melissa, *there* you are," the petite, blonde-haired lady admonished lightly, taking the little girl by the hand. "Come on. We need to get on. Visiting hours are almost over."

The little one resisted the pull of the adult's hand for one more moment to gaze in to the room before succumbing to the tug to head down the hallway and in to a different direction.

Coming Soon

Bramden House: Future's Crossing

www.ingramcontent.com/pod-product-compliance
Lightning Source LLC
Chambersburg PA
CBHW070459260626
47161CB00004B/1368

* 9 7 9 8 9 8 9 2 4 5 1 3 0 *